His Own Master

His Own Master

A. Z. WRIGHT

LUTE PUBLISHING

This first edition published in 2017

1 3 5 7 9 10 8 6 4 2

ISBN 978-0-9931453-1-5

Typeset by Deltatype Ltd, Birkenhead, Merseyside
Printed in Great Britain by Biddles Books Ltd

for Lute Publishing

Contents

CHAPTER I

'Wincanton is a parish and Market town in the hundred of Norton Ferris, county of Somerset, 108 miles W. by S. of London; it is governed by the magistrates of the county, and is pleasantly situated on the gradual declivity of a hill; the town consists of five streets, many of the houses are well and substantially built and have a handsome appearance, there is a market held every Wednesday, and fairs annually on the Tuesday in Easter week and September 29th. There are also some excellent inns. The surrounding country is extremely fertile and well cultivated, on the turnpike road leading to Dorset, the view ranges over a wide extent, the air is considered extremely salubrious, and the pleasantness of hotels, render Wincanton as pleasant and agreeable a place of residence as any in the country.'

So is described the town of Wincanton in Somerset, in a trades directory of the late 1840s. To this description there follow the names of the inhabitants of note; that is to say, the gentry and clergy. Below this, a firm dividing line is drawn, under which is displayed a listing of the recognised traders and their businesses within the area. Included in this listing is an iron foundry, owned by one Oliver Maggs and located out in the village of Bourton, some four miles from Wincanton, in the county of

Dorset. It stands a little way along a winding upward pathway leading northwards from the main street of the village, aptly known as factory hill. Beside it lies a factory pond. Adjacent to it is a flax mill, part owned by Oliver Maggs and which is powered by the largest waterwheel in Europe: sixty feet in diameter and four feet wide. Some of the workers at the mill reside at Twine Cottage, not fifty yards away, in rather overcrowded conditions. Oliver Maggs lives within the immediate vicinity, occupying an expansive house by the name of Bullpits, overlooking the factories from an elevated position on the other side of the pond. Unlike the foundry men at Nant-y-glô, who have resorted to strikes and rioting, the workers at Bourton seem content with their lot, allowing Oliver Maggs and his family to live continually in an atmosphere of peace and harmony, without fear of attack on their persons or of ever knowing poverty. But some are more content than others: for the sake of accuracy, I should have revealed that there was an apprentice iron founder by the name of Sam Brazenall who had been verging on discontentment for the entire course of his twenty-one years. At around half-past five of this mild day in March 1849, he was coming to the end of his working day at the iron foundry at Bourton. He had worked solidly all afternoon, for his afternoon tea-break had been sacrificed for the privilege of leaving half-an-hour early. Ideally, he would have preferred both to have a tea break and leave early, but his overseer was unsympathetic to that approach. What was initially a twelve hour day was already reduced to a ten hour day should the lunch break and tea breaks be taken into account. Asking for yet more free time would be well frowned upon.

The smoky, clay atmosphere that always permeated the interior of the foundry had been unusually thick that day. Within the space of eleven hours, Sam had created over forty iron casts. The work was hot and dusty, hard and repetitive. There were some days that he felt he could stand it no longer. Today was such a day. As if reading his thoughts, a voice behind him suddenly distracted him.

"You can be off now". Sam turned from the box that he had just filled and firmly packed with sand. His overseer seemed to want him to go, for some reason, although there was still another five minutes of working time left. He came out of the dark, gloomy foundry and into the fading daylight. He made his way down the winding factory hill, under a leafy shade alongside the mill stream, crossing over the little bridge. As he turned into the main thoroughfare, he was passed by the Yeovil coach, trundling noisily along at what could be no more than five miles an hour along the bumpy road. A stranger might have thought twice about walking along this road, for it had always been footpad territory. But to Sam, with empty pockets and known to all prospective local highwaymen, it presented no such threats. He walked on, with ease. The Red Lion stood up ahead on his left, just before the road rose out of Bourton. His mother liked him to come straight home for dinner, but sometimes he could not resist stopping off there for half an hour. In this place, a safe distance from his home, he would consume a liberal quantity of beer, before finally continuing along the road. He had long since developed a taste for drink, for the inn was kept by his uncle; he had drunk there since he was thirteen. When he drank, a sudden feeling of control and superiority would overcome him;

though when he drank heavily, the drink would take all the work out of him the next day. It was as much as he could manage for him to work at all. Work was such a burden to him, so unnatural and pointless. If it were not for his father's continual pressure, he would have bolted for the second time from his apprenticeship, never mind the ensuing prison sentence.

The inn was bright and well kept, with flowering vegetation all over one end. On reaching the modern building, Sam stepped unhesitatingly past one of its solid oak doors. It would be twilight by the time he came out again. There were not many inside - most of the men were still working. He crossed over the light oak floorboards over to his usual seat, a narrow bench by one window. Marge appeared.

"What'll it be, beer or gin?"

Marge really wasn't a very good bar maid, Sam always thought. She looked more like a governess. The trouble was she didn't talk like one.

"Beer. I've acquired a distaste for gin."

"Verry sensible. There's nothing 'cept poison innit."

I wish she'd change that dress, thought Sam. It seemed inappropriate that a governess should be wearing red with white polka dots. But when the beer arrived, he went into a better mood.

"So yer coming to the end of yer apprenticeship, now," said Marge, hovering around as usual.

"That's right, Marge. And I'm not pained by that either."

"Yer'll soon be earning a decent living then. Like yer father."

Sam continued to swig beer until the jug was empty.

He placed it heavily down upon the rough wooden table before him. Marge took it immediately.

"I won't be here much longer, Marge," said Sam.

"Oh? Where you going then?"

"Wales, most like."

"Wales? Do they have iron founders there?"

"Well, they must do."

"Yes, well, I suppose if they have iron they must have iron founders. I wish I could just take off, like that."

"You could, Marge."

"Oh, I wouldn't know how to keep meself. You're lucky, being a man. Being able to keep yerself."

"I don't know about that, Marge," said Sam, quietly. He had just made the decision that he would go to Wales. The idea had been vaguely brewing for some time, but now it was irrevocable. He had always wondered about other parts; during his more leisurely earlier life at the day school in town he had been taught geography; yet so far he had seen only Somersetshire and not too much of that either. Apart from the immediate vicinity of Wincanton, the only other place that he could remember was the town of Crewkerne, the place to where he had bolted during the course of his apprenticeship. That was four years ago. His overseer had ordered him to do more than his allotted work, and he had remonstrated, only to be told that he was idle and useless. The following morning on leaving the house he had turned right along the road leading to Yeovil instead of left, towards Bourton and the factory. Walking all day, he had arrived in Yeovil in the afternoon and had drunk all evening in the town. During the night he had slept in a haystack in a nearby field. The following day he had been off on the road again with the rising sun. Feeling hungry, he had bought bread and cheese on the way with the few coins that he had left and then they were gone. On arrival in Crewkerne, he had come to the iron foundry and asked for work there. This he had got. Three days later, his brother turned up with a special constable. His father had found out where he was and had sent them to bring him back. After that he was told to behave himself or go to prison. For nearly five years he had been a normal labouring man, up at five, home at six, and was likely to stay in such a state. But the end of his apprenticeship was approaching; it was a mere matter of weeks away. When the time finally came, it would be nice to shake a free leg and see a little of life. He would tell his father that as an apprentice who had served his time, he would go to Wales to find work. His father would never know that he had no intention of working, but wanted just to see Wales. With any luck his father would give him the money for the coach to Bristol and perhaps a bit more. As he became drowsier and more invigorated, the plan settled itself into a more real and concrete form. Freedom was in sight.

"Can yer hear me, Sam?"

Sam came to and looked up; Marge was standing over him again. "Yer'll 'ave to pay for the next one, I'm afraid."

"Oh," said Sam. He reached hurriedly into his trouser pockets.

"I've only a penny, Marge."

"That'll do for the moment. I don't think yer uncle will give you beer for nothing when you're working proper, though."

Well, I won't be here, thought Sam. It was exciting to think that in twenty or so days he would not be in

6

Wincanton. Men were now starting to trickle into the inn, to try to capture a few hours of entertainment before the day's end. They were unsmiling and tired, shabby and drab. Sam took a final gulp of his beer and stood up. He made his way past the men, who stood about, murmuring.

"Sam," called out a voice, suddenly.

Sam turned to locate the man who was addressing him – it was Thomas Dawes, a flax spinner, who worked in the shoe-thread manufactory, adjacent to the iron foundry. "Hello, Tom. How do you get on?"

"Oh, not so bad. Musn't grumble. The wife won't let me grumble. Though you look cheerful, more cheerful than usual, if I may say so."

"Do I? It must be the prospect of leaving these parts."

"Leaving these parts? You'll be lucky!" Tom drank down half his beer.

"What do you mean?"

"Well, look what happened the last time."

"I was bound to my apprenticeship, then. My apprenticeship is nearly up."

"I know it is. But you'll still be working for your master."

"Not on your life."

"Well, who are you going to work for, then?"

"No one round here."

"Where are you going? Not back to Crewkerne, I presume."

"No. I'm going to Wales."

"Wales? What's so grand about Wales?"

"It's a place I'd like to see."

"Well, you won't be seeing much of it, stuck in one

of their grim foundries," concluded Tom, downing the remainder of his beer. With this piece of insight, he disappeared back into the crowd. Sam sighed.

The late evening was rapidly drawing in. Thoughts of home began to creep into Sam's mind; he could see his mother, fretting herself over his absence at the table, and his father, shouting tyrannically at his brothers and sisters or lapsing into taciturnity. Perhaps he had better not stay out any later. He strode out, leaving the pub and its attempt at gaiety behind him, and trudged upwards along the road, towards the oversized setting sun. He passed the church, standing in front of a wide open landscape. It was a mile and a half to By-The-Way Cottage, where he was allowed to live through the courtesy of his father. The cottage was situated more or less exactly where the Dorset – Somerset border lay – he could not be sure to which county he belonged.

Once over the rise, the road stretched ahead of him, downwards then upwards. He could make out a black covered mail wagon approaching him from the bottom, heading for the villages between Wincanton and Mere. In order to save the horse, the driver had dismounted and was walking dejectedly along beside the wagon. It all looked rather pathetic, he thought. It did not compare with the sight of a Royal Mail coach, decorated in black and scarlet, tearing along the highway at night between Yeovil and Salisbury. He remembered how, as a child, he had wanted to be a mail guard and stand at the back of the coach armed with a blunderbuss and two pistols. No highwayman ever dared to attack a mail coach. The mail guard also got to blow a melodious coach horn, to advise other road users of their fast approach, or to alert the post house of the imminent arrival of the coach, or to warn tollgate keepers to open the gate. Lagging behind the times, the Yeovil to Salisbury coach still ran twice daily.

As the wagon perambulated past, Sam looked sympathetically towards the mail carrier.

"They'll be the death of me, these hills," declared the man. He appeared very poor and unfit for the job.

"Me too," said Sam, most sincerely. He felt trapped in a circle, that forever took him from Bourton to By-The-Way Cottage, or By-The-Way Cottage to Wincanton, or back again. If it did not kill him it would certainly drive him insane. The resolve to go to Wales became even stronger. The wagon passed and he walked on, up a hill again and over a plateau; the far distant hazy landscape of fields and meadows came into view just as the road fell again, on its approach to Leigh Common. Down below, alongside the roadway, stood a smart new building named by its owner as The Hunter's Lodge. Here, men of exalted status would revive their spirits after a morning of shooting, conversing on matters irrelevant to the daily necessities of life. Such a life would suit me admirably, thought Sam; to think that he lived so close to these gentlemen and was yet so far away from them. It was only chance that had put him in Bourton Foundry and the gentlemen in The Hunter's Lodge. They were free to do anything they chose and took orders from no one other than the queen. Finally, when sick of each other's company and their country pleasures, they would pack their bags and leave. But so soon will I, thought Sam; for twenty-one years he had lived on a road down which many coaches and carriers passed; soon he himself would finally be passing through. Wincanton was not a place in which the traveller wished to remain for long, and Sam did not wish to remain there any longer either. He himself would soon become a traveller, and there was no mode of existence that Sam could imagine to be more pleasurable.

By-The-Way Cottage was on the same side of the road, a little further on. It was of a very reasonable size and was sort of able to accommodate the fourteen family members inhabiting it. There were four windows at the front and none on the side. It was partially obscured by an overgrown hedge. To enter it, you walked through an iron archway covered in leafy branches bending over and entwining each other, down a little path through a front garden and up to the porch. To the side of the house was a small enclosed grassy area, overshadowed by a great tree, where a couple of hens ran about. The house was always in good repair; it was always adequately heated and lit. Sam's father was paid thirty-five shillings a week as a clerk at the flax mill in Bourton and his house, coals and candles had found him. On no occasion had Sam experienced prolonged hunger or cold. Though despite the comforts provided by his father, Sam liked his mother best; his father's harsh words always drove any thoughts of right and wrong out of his head. As he was about to enter the house, he reassured himself that the hour was still before seven. Opening the unlocked door, he was immediately confronted by the lord of the manor, emerging from the parlour.

"Out drinking again," the older man growled. "You've missed tea – and you won't get any either."

"What if I have?" Sam walked nonchalantly past the ill-tempered man in white shirt sleeves who purported to be his father and went upstairs. It was his drinking that always seemed to send the man into a rage. He was only half an hour late home and had only had two pints. He opened a door and stepped inside a narrow, darkened room. A brother, the same brother who had brought him back from Crewkerne, was lying on the bed at the opposite wall, not three feet away. Daniel was sickly and always ailing from something or other.

"What's the matter now, Daniel?"

"I have a headache."

"Oh, not again," said Sam, sitting down on his bed. "It's all those books you read."

"Nothing to do with it. You might like to read a few books yourself, Sam. And I don't mean Dick Turpin or Jack Shepherd."

"I don't think that will get me anywhere, do you?"

"Well, perhaps not. You're more the stalwart labouring type, I suppose."

Sam lit the candle on the table beside and threw himself back on his bed.

"Oh, please put that out, Sam," said Daniel, at once. "I'm trying to sleep."

"How did you grow up so namby-pamby, Daniel?" Sam snuffed out the candle with two fingers. When the night drew in, his mother came into the room. She was always caring and nervous. Her dress, though made from a simple cloth, was always clean and without rends.

"Sam, come and have some tea. I saved some for you."

Sam got up. He hopped down the narrow, steep staircase like a mountain goat and went to his place at the long table in the parlour. At its head was seated his father. Sam sighed. But instead of the tirade that Sam was expecting, the man just sat and stared at him in silence. His mother placed a pie before him; Sam began to eat, ignoring his father's stare. The baby upstairs began to cry.

"Sam, I have given you a home ever since you were a child," his father began. "But in three weeks time, you will have a trade at your fingers' ends. You will be able to provide for yourself."

"I suppose that's true," said Sam.

"I want you to leave home," continued his father. Sam glanced at him quickly.

"Why?" he asked.

"I have too many children in this house without worrying about you as well."

Sam continued to eat and did not look again at the man who was speaking so harshly to him. It made no difference now, anyway. He had already made up his mind to leave.

"Well, if I have to go, then I have to go," he said, resignedly.

"You see, Thomas, Sam has grown into a man," said his mother, suddenly. "He may have gone astray as a boy but now he has reformed himself. You must give him a little money, to start him off." Upstairs, the baby began to cry again; she turned and left the parlour. Sam could not remember a time when he had not continually heard babies crying in the house.

Sam looked at his father. "I would prefer to find work outside Somerset," he said, continuing to eat voraciously. "I've had enough of round here. And like you said, I can provide for myself. I can work elsewhere just as easily as here." There was a silence, which his father eventually broke.

"Well, as long as you are not living here, I don't care where you work. Where are you intending to work?"

"I thought Wales."

"Wales?"

"Yes. But it might take me two weeks to travel there and find work."

"And how do you propose to support yourself during that time? Not to mention the cost of getting there."

Sam did not answer.

"I will give you four pounds," said his father, finally. "That should cover everything."

"More than everything, father."

Sam consumed the rest of his meal in silence. There did not seem to be anything else to say. His father got up from the wooden table just as his mother returned. She appeared anxious. The man walked past his mother and upstairs. As his mother collected up the supper plate, she said, quietly,

"I hope you do not feel harshly treated. I did not want you to leave, but it is no use you trying to stay. He will not change his mind, I know it."

"Don't worry, mother. I can manage."

"I would have liked you to have been a better scholar," his mother went on. "And I'm sure you could have if you hadn't neglected your studies. Your father paid fifteen shillings a year for five years to keep you at the day school in Wincanton…"

"Yes, I know, mother, but it's no good you telling me that now."

"Well, let's hope you make good."

Sam would have liked to go out for another drink. However, he felt that he couldn't, for it would upset his mother and vex his father. How he longed to leave home! Then he would be able to drink as much as he pleased, without anyone saying anything about it. He hopped up the steep staircase again, the steps of which were not deep enough for a whole foot. Tomorrow would be Saturday, a short, nine-hour day, followed by a day of rest. Stopping at home and bringing himself to work had been such a burden for too long. Now escape was in sight. Inside his room again, Daniel did not stir. Sam fell exhausted onto his bed. Within a minute slumber overcame him in its usual pleasant fashion from which he would not awake until half-past five when in the distance, the factory bell would ring out its terrible peal. Only for three more weeks would he suffer its torment – in three weeks he would be far away, released from the shackles of his labour and the monotony of his home.

CHAPTER 2

Sam considered that he had acquired no more knowledge during the last three years of his apprenticeship than he had in the first two. He had learnt most things, but one thing he was sure he could not learn was to get on with Aaron. Aaron was his co-worker. He was therefore obliged to exist nearly twelve hours a day within ten yards of a highly uncongenial man. The first year had been insufferable; Aaron had been his immediate superior, and he had had to take every order that the man had thrown at him. This had been the cause of his bolting to Crewkerne.

"So you're off, then," said Aaron, as Sam planted air holes in an infinitely practised fashion into the sand packing of the mould he was working on.

Sam turned to look at the rough man. It was very unusual for Aaron to speak to him unprompted.

"Yes," responded Sam, in surprise.

"Found work somewhere else?"

"I will do."

"Well, I can't say I'm going to miss you."

Sam could not even move himself to retort. Nothing Aaron said mattered any more, now. He could suffer anything that the man subjected him to, for it had no relevance to his future. He now thought only of the future, for it looked brighter than ever before. The vision that dominated his mind now was of that day, a Wednesday, in eighteen days time, when he would walk out of the house and take the road to Wincanton for the last time; his eleven brothers and sisters would wave to him from the cottage windows, his mother would stand watching at the door. They would possibly never see him again, and probably would not care. One more empty bed, that was how they looked at it. Well, they were welcome to it. He would soon be far away. From the Bear in Wincanton, he would take the coach to Bath and then the train to Bristol. From Bristol, he would take a packet to Wales.

At around eight the bell sounded, and the men knocked off instantly. Sam sat down with his breakfast – bread, cheese and a can of coffee. The coffee was kept warm by the furnace. It was a most welcome tonic; without it, Sam could never have kept going for the rest of the morning. Aaron always sat away from him in his own cocoon. Sam continued to find him to be a dull, energetic man, reluctant to converse and with an absolute abhorrence for anything of a hypothetical nature. The repetitiveness of the work seemed not to faze him at all and the two hundred or so moulds that he churned out per week were to him no more than hard work. Sam sometimes wondered what sort of thoughts passed through the man's head, if any. One bone of contention was that Aaron had found out that Sam could read. His attitude towards Sam was one of contempt, suspicion and ridicule. In return, Sam had taken to view the man as nothing more than a piece of furniture. In this way had they been interacting for five whole years; the entire extent of Sam's apprenticeship. It had begun that way and looked as thought it was going to end that way. But perhaps, thought Sam, as their acquaintance was soon to end, an attempt at civility should be made. Though judging from Aaron's expression now might not be the ideal time.

Half-an-hour later, the factory bell rang out again. That meant, 'time's up now, not five minutes from now.' Sam put down the coffee. He had during the first two hours already completed about eight castings; all small, miscellaneous items. He and Aaron always seemed to be assigned the 'jobbing' castings. The owner of 'The Greyhound' in Wincanton wanted a new iron sign for the inn. What was more, they wanted it tomorrow. Were they not to get it by the agreed time, he or Aaron might be fined.

The sign would require a large size mould. The heavy, two-piece box that served as the frame for the mould was on the floor before him. He sprinkled it with a covering of chalk; then he began shovelling in the sand and clay mixture beside him. With a hammer, he packed in the sand very densely then shovelled in more sand. When the mould was finally prepared, Sam looked over his shoulder to see Aaron standing by the tall, cylindrical cupola at the back of the foundry. It was within this artistic construction that pig-iron, fresh from the furnace was melted down. All the moulding-boxes that the men had prepared that morning and the day before were on the floor of the foundry, ready for casting. Some of them were very large; some so large that a box had not been used, and the item would be cast directly onto sand on the floor. Sam went over to Aaron and helped pour the blindingly bright orange liquid into a pail. Then, on cue, Sam picked up his end of the ladle and carried the pail over to the casting moulds that he and Aaron had created.

There, with care and attention, they poured the molten iron in through the hole at the top of each mould, until the box was full, moving down the line. And so the day dragged on.

Just before noon, when they were about to knock off for lunch, Sam asked of Aaron,

"Have you ever been to Newport?"

"Never heard of it."

"It's a port in Wales. You can get there by steam packet from Bristol."

Aaron slung his eating bag over his shoulder and ambled off out of the dark foundry. Sam followed him outside into the salubrious air to the factory pond round the back of the factories. There, on the banks of its still, green waters, others from the flax mill were also sitting and eating. Sam wished he could leave there and then but realized it could not be done. He would sit out the three weeks, thereby arousing no suspicions. He walked over to Aaron. The man was staring out at the opposite side of the pond, a sandwich in his mouth.

"I wonder what this place will be like in a hundred years' time," mused Sam. "Do you think the factories and the pond will still be here?"

"I don't know what you're talking about," said Aaron. Sam stepped away from him again and opened his own eating bag. His mother was always very conscientious with his lunch; never could he complain that he had not enough to eat. He took out from the bag the pie and flask that was always provided and sat down on the grassy area that lay all around. The machinery of the shoe-thread manufactory was quiet now, as it would be for an hour; now the ambient sounds of birdsong, stream and breeze rustling through the leaves prevailed. Soon the machinery would return to its continual, repetitive drone. Sam could not wait for the day when he would never hear it again; but time seemed to be dragging; he now realised that the coming three weeks were going to feel long and hard. Every minute seemed to have to be worked through. Twenty minutes of sitting by the pond seemed like two hours. He tried not to think about time passing, but that was all he could think about.

What would Wales be like, he wondered. Not that it mattered. As long as he was able to do as he liked, just for once. Without the burden of work, there would be time to relax, drink and look around the place. It would be easy enough to be happy anywhere as long as it was away from here. If only he could just get moving ... The factory bell rang out again. Lolling on the grassy ground, Sam watched as the flax workers stood up in a slow, reluctant fashion and trudged back into their prison. Sam stood up and went into the foundry again after Aaron. Only another two hours, he consoled himself. For it was Saturday, the short day. It was also payday – that was to say, payday for his mother – all Sam did was collect the money to give to her. She would expect him to come straight home. But with luck, he could probably go out to The Red Lion or The Unicorn in the nearby village of Bayford some time in the evening, when his father was not looking. He was beginning to have that Saturday feeling. Finally, he stood up to follow the others, and went back in, a full thirty seconds late.

"Last, as usual," said Mr Exon, watching him as he walked over to the bench; but the overseer did not appear to require a response, so Sam did not give one. He immediately got to work. Mr Exon went back into the machine room, apparently satisfied with his behaviour.

He was home by three in the afternoon. Standing in the parlour, amongst his rowdy siblings, he gave his mother the seven shillings that he had caused to pass from Oliver Maggs to her roughened hands.

"Thank you, Sam," she said, as she always did, dropping the silver coins into the money-box that always stood upon the mantel shelf. But as always there was something in her tone that suggested that she knew he didn't want to give her the money, but would rather have spent it on drink. She turned towards him again.

"I have put together some money to buy you a suit," she said, unexpectedly. "Your Sunday clothes are looking a bit sad. You must appear fit for employment when you seek work in Wales. Though nothing too fine, just a plain, black suit; we don't want you looking like a dandy."

How thoughtful, thought Sam. She was right. His so-called Sunday Best was not what it should be.

"You will go to Dowding in the High Street," went on his mother. "I have already instructed him to supply you with a suit of cotton. All that he requires now is your measurements."

"I shall find time to go sometime next week," said Sam. "After work."

"I do not want you out on the streets of Wincanton late in the evening," said his mother. "You had better go now."

Sam walked towards the door again.

"And mind you come straight back. Your father will be home soon."

Without reply, Sam came out of the house and set off

along the road again. It fell downwards and towards the left, amidst trees on either side. The distance to Wincanton was two miles; he should be in the High Street in a little over half an hour. Sam thought he knew every inch of these two miles; he had been forced to walk them six days a week to attend the National School in Wincanton from the age of eight to between twelve and thirteen. His mind flew back to the first day at school, where he had made the acquaintance of Miss West, junior mistress. She had inaugurated herself with a speech, which Sam could remember as if it were yesterday.

"You are a working-class child and can live only by working. Society has an order, and you must accept your place in the order of society. You must respect your elders and betters. Your betters are Miss West, The Reverend Dodsworth, and Doctor Flack."

After this had been made clear the long, dusky days had passed in the recitation of multiplication tables, spelling, and the catechism, for what ever use it was. His reports had not been good; on many occasions had Miss West been obliged to reprimand him. In time he had moved up to the senior school; this was taught by a man not unlike himself in many ways. In these years, however, his attendance had dwindled, and he had passed many a lazy hour in places other than the schoolroom. Away from the dictates of the master, it was then that his drinking habit had taken hold. He had as yet no desire to be released from its chain.

Quickening his pace, he walked on along the winding and undulating road. The trees soon disappeared to reveal wide-ranging views of the vale on either side. The sky ahead of him was a dull white; the air was rather cool.

There was virtually no traffic on the way; as he passed through the hamlet of Bayford, the Unicorn was just opening, early on a Saturday. From Bayford, the road ran for a mile straight down the hill into the High Street of Wincanton, on either side of which were many inns and shops. Most of the shops were closed, but for a couple. However, the gas lights all along the street were not yet lit. People were milling about or loitering on the pavements. The tailor was right at the other end of the street, he knew. He kept on walking down the incline upon which the town was built, and on the approach towards its juncture with North Street, to his horror he could unmistakeably make out the familiar figure of Miss West, advancing up the hill towards him in her usual, elephantine gait. She appeared to have dispensed with the use of a corset. She had undoubtedly just turned in from North Street; the National School was situated a little way down it. Sam usually managed to keep out of his old mistress' way, but this time she appeared to have him cornered.

"Master Brazenall! I hope you haven't come into town to drink, this early in the afternoon."

Well, what if I have, thought Sam. Do you honestly think I care at all what you think? He tried to keep his expression reasonably pleasant.

` "No, not at all. I have to see a tailor. My mother wants me to have a new suit."

"A new suit? Are you starting a job?"

"Well, yes, I should be, soon."

A superior, triumphant look passed briefly over Miss West's no-nonsense features.

"I knew we could make a man of you, and we did," she said, in a sure tone. "You were a difficult one, I admit, but you came round in the end. My only regret is that you did not progress as far as we hoped you would. Well, it doesn't really matter now."

You don't matter now, thought Sam.

"Where is this job?" she asked, looking up at him, as she was now obliged to do, owing to their relative heights.

"It's in Wales," replied Sam.

"Oh," said the woman, dubiously. "That's a long way away."

"I'm glad to say that it is."

"Well, as long as you're working, that's the main thing."

"Yes," agreed Sam. "Look here, I'm afraid I'm in a bit of a hurry. The tailor's waiting especially for me, see? I really have to go."

"Oh. Well, if I don't see you again, I shall think of you, working hard at your new job. Goodbye, Sam." And she moved on past him.

Well, that wasn't too bad, breathed Sam. Though he really should be more careful when coming close to the school. He rarely walked past it, for the sight of its bare windows and sandy brick walls would conjure up atmospheres of discipline once induced by that now seemingly diminutive woman. Sam tried to dismiss her immediately from his mind but failed; the feeling of discomfort continued to irk him right until he reached the purposely elegant doors of the tailor, on the other side of the street.

A jangling bell rang out as Sam entered the gloomy shop; racks of half-made suits and shirts hung all around. Almost immediately an efficient-looking man appeared as if from nowhere.

"Can I help you, Sir?" the man enquired.

"I'm Sam Brazenall. My mother sent me here to be measured up for a suit."

"Oh, yes. Well, step this way, Sir,"

Sam followed the man's dainty steps towards a door at the back of the shop. As he did so, he could not help but notice a sorrowful worker in one corner, badly lit by candlelight, beside some half-made garments. Sam knew that the work would not be finished until the late evening or well into the night. At least his own suit would not be required the next day; the poor man would have three weeks to make it. The man looked briefly up at Sam. But Sam disappeared into the parlour whereupon the tailor measured him at lightning speed. The ordeal over, Sam was able to leave the shop less than three minutes after he had walked in. It was still fairly light outside. The clock on the town hall tower displayed the time to be a quarter past four. The Bear would be open. But he had no money to buy drink. He would be obliged to return home. He began trudging up the hill again, in the opposite direction. Perhaps he could get out to The Red Lion after supper.

On the day of rest, Sam woke at 8 a.m. but wished to return to sleep again. He vaguely saw and heard his mother enter the room, to remind him of church. No, he thought, decisively. No church today. It was too much, having to listen to an opinionated, ranting preacher, who always went on over his time. Even from the safety of his bed, Sam could hear in his head the insignificant man's insistent words. 'A little sleep, a little slumber, a little folding of the hands to rest – and poverty will come on you like a bandit and scarcity like an armed man.' Well, a little sleep and a little slumber were just what he felt like, right now. He turned over, pulling up the covers. But as sleep enveloped him once more, he was re-awoken by Daniel, shaking him and pulling the blankets back off him.

"We're all waiting for you, Sam." Sam forced his eyes open to view his pathetic brother standing over him. He got out of bed and went to the sideboard in the corner of the room, where he quickly poured water from a jug into the porcelain bowl.

"I'll be down in a minute, Daniel," he said, splashing the freezing water onto his face.

Daniel left, leaving Sam alone in the tiny bedroom. He was not often alone and the few minutes of solitude were of value to him. Only when alone did he think the greatest of thoughts. And now more thoughts of the future were coming to him. When he was finally away, he would not go near any church. He took down the fustian jacket and corduroy trousers that hung over a chair and donned them; his new suit was not ready yet, but even when it was, he would not wear it, keeping it in pristine condition until his impending voyage of discovery.

The family, minus the babies and toddlers, was standing in a group outside. Sister Margaret would stay to mind them. Then they walked off slowly over Leigh Common towards Stoke Church, a mile away. The grass was dewy; Sam's boots immediately became wet. But that was better than being muddy.

On arrival at the church, they all found their way to their allotted places in a pew near the back. Sam was sitting at the end, next to Daniel. Shortly afterwards, the vicar came out of the vestry, but today it was a different vicar; Sam had never seen him before. Instead of the doddery old man dressed in black, a younger, brighter man, adorned in violet was now stepping up into the pulpit. The low murmur in the church immediately died down.

"Hymn number three hundred and forty-seven," the impressive new figure began.

The entire congregation began to bawl out in unison a harsh, tuneless number. Sam never bothered singing; he could never enter into the spirit of these things. He just listened to Daniel's passable tenor voice, audible above the cacophony. Finally, all six verses were got through. There was a scuffling as the people sat down again. Then there was silence. The bright, young man looked up around him briefly, then began to speak:

"This above all: to thine own self be true. And it must follow, as the night the day, Thou canst not then be false to any man. These are the words of William Shakespeare, and they represent the true nature of honesty. Only when you are honest with yourself can you be honest with others." He paused, momentously. Someone in the middle of the congregation coughed.

"Only when you are true to yourself will you find your true place in life," went on the vicar. "Only when you are true to yourself will you cease to let yourself and others down."

What has happened to the usual vicar, wondered Sam. This new priest seemed to have an impetus that was most inspiring; his resonant voice rang out with ardour, echoing around the church; the bulky bible, which would lie always open in front of the preacher, remained closed throughout the sermon. Instead of falling asleep as he usually did on these occasions, Sam continued to listen;

the manner in which the sermon was delivered was quite overwhelming. Such rhetoric was previously unknown in these parts. Nor was it too long; it could not have been more than ten minutes: a short sermon if ever there was one. And as the new man of the cloth proposed the second hymn for the day, his words continued to ring out through Sam's head: to thine own self be true. Well, that was exactly what he was doing. He wanted to get away, and he was getting away. A life of drudgery in the foundry was something he could never subject himself to. If the rest of society and his family wished to lead such a life, that was their business, but it was not for him. It had just taken that one decision; not even the most plausible of arguments would stop him now. But he would not inform anyone of his intentions all the same. In their narrow-minded way, they would most surely not approve. Anyone other than the new vicar, that was. He thought briefly of making the acquaintance of this interesting person after the service but then thought better of it. His family was there, and that would make things awkward. No, he decided; for his remaining time in Somerset, it would be better to blend into the background as much as possible. As the congregation knelt in prayer, his analysis was interrupted by Daniel's urgent whisper:

"Sam!"

"What is it?"

"What day are you leaving?"

"The Wednesday after Easter."

"Are you taking your spelling book with you?"

"No. Why, do you want it?"

"Yes."

"I suppose you can have it. It doesn't look as though I

will be coming back."

"Thanks, Sam."

The inevitable disapproving hush from his mother caused them both to turn their heads to the floor. They would soon be out in the daylight again and walking back to the cottage for the usual ritual of Sunday lunch, followed by the monologues of visitors. One more time did Sam count the number of days that would have to pass before he was free to leave and found there to be only one less than there had been the day before.

CHAPTER 3

On the morning of his departure, Sam stood inside the house, by the open front door framing the bright spring day without. The London to Bath stage coach would pass by in less than two hours time. He wore the fustian jacket and corduroy trousers that had for many years constituted his Sunday Best. His new suit was folded up in his bag of clothes.

"Where exactly in Wales was it you said you were going, Sam?" asked his mother, hovering anxiously in the hallway.

"Newport, mother."

"Newport? Do they have foundries there?"

"Oh, yes. All down by the docks, they do."

"How do you know?"

"Well, how are they going to build and repair ships, otherwise? You need millions of nails to build a ship."

"Yes, I suppose you do. Are you going there by ship?"

"Yes. I'm taking the steam packet from Bristol."

"Well, you should have enough with you to eat until you get to Bristol," said his mother. "I wouldn't try to eat what they give you on the boat; it won't be palatable. I hope the passage will not be too rough. I have heard that the Bristol Channel can be very stormy."

"It won't bother me, mother. Don't concern yourself."

"And be careful not to lose your bag on the boat. There will be many thieves about."

"I shall, mother."

His mother approached him. "Well, I am sure you cannot fail to find work in your new suit, and bearing your certificate of apprenticeship," she said, with confidence. "You will soon feel strong and independent."

"Yes," agreed Sam, wholeheartedly.

His mother went back into the kitchen. His father was at work now, but that morning at around five a.m. in the parlour the authoritarian figure had presented his eldest son with the sum of three pounds ten shillings, and unexpectedly, a watch.

"You must always have a watch, to prove your worth," he had said, in a most earnest tone. "For the absence of a watch is the first sure sign of bankruptcy." With these final words, the older and wiser man had taken his immediate leave.

As he stood in the hallway, Sam brought out the watch from his corduroy pocket and examined it again. It looked as though it might have been quite valuable at one time, perhaps even so now, for there were not too many scratches on its silver pair case. With one hand, Sam opened it for the second time, to view the dial, colourfully painted to show the changing of the guard. The delicate hour and minute hand were attached to a castle tower, at the base of which an arched doorway was pierced to reveal ivory disc. It was, according to this neat timepiece, five and twenty minutes past eleven; still another hour to go. But now, he had a desire to get away as fast as he could. It would be better to walk to the Bear in Wincanton and catch the stagecoach from there instead.

Sam slipped the watch back into his pocket and picked up his bag of clothes.

"Bye, Mother," he called out.

His mother reappeared again.

"Are you going already, Sam?"

"Yes. Haven't got a minute to lose."

Sam walked out of the house. Through the garden path he went, under the verdant archway and out onto the road. An easterly wind blew with him as he took the first few steps away from home. Looking behind him briefly, he saw two of his younger siblings, still infants, staring at him bemusedly from the garden gate. He quickened his pace and walked rapidly away from Leigh Common, along the old, familiar route towards the town.

He arrived in Wincanton in record time. It was just noon as he came up to the Bear Inn. Inside all was stir and bustle, with doors opening and shutting, bells ringing, voices calling out to the waiter from every quarter. Sam sat down in an unfamiliar state of relaxation, looking vainly around for someone to serve him. He took another look at his watch; it was five past twelve. The coach was due in an hour. When a waiter finally materialised, he ordered a pint of ale. This is the life for me, he thought, wondering why he had been kept from it for so long. When his glass was empty, he ordered another beer, then another. It was only a shilling gone. At a quarter to one he walked out again, to see the stagecoach to Bath rattling through the archway into the yard behind. It pulled abruptly to a halt, whereupon the driver immediately jumped down from his high seat and opened the door of the coach. Four men and two women, dressed in hardy travelling clothes, stepped carefully out. They hurried inside the inn as the ostlers came out to change the horses. For this service, they would be expected to give tips all round, including to the driver and post-boy. Perhaps travelling by coach was not such a good idea after all. At 3d a mile for twenty-three miles plus tips, the journey would cost him no less than six shillings. What was more, the coach appeared crowded. It would not be such a long walk to Bristol; the day was mild, and the Northern road would be in quite good condition. Sam decided not to take the coach after all. He left the inn and went off; it was necessary to walk down North Street and past The National School, but he was met by no one. The houses very quickly began to disperse until there were only a couple and then it was just open landscape again. The road stretched invitingly before him. With a spring in his step, he headed outwards along a winding, endless path, down deep green avenues and past dark orchards, not once regretting having forgone the questionable convenience of the stuffy stage-coach. He was observed by no overseer, no one was there to direct his movements. Never before had he been so completely free; his bag felt light; he kept walking on away from Wincanton, stopping leisurely here and there to eat or drink, sitting on a gate, or in a meadow by a stream, in the company of a herd of cows. How nice it was not to be in the factory. He thought of Aaron, mechanically working on throughout the day, always reliable, never tired or jaded. But after one such break, as he stood up again to move on, all thoughts of home suddenly left him. There would be a packet from Bristol to Newport the following day, in the morning or afternoon. Where should he spend the night? Perhaps it would be best to sleep in a field outside Bristol – it was not yet very cold, and the grass was not really damp. Sam took the money out of his pocket again – it correctly amounted to £3 9s. How much would the packet fare be? Not more than the price of a coach, surely? Climbing back over the stile, he wandered on, still meeting no one until half-an-hour later, when from the distance, a cart, pulled arduously along by a pack horse and laden with apples and cabbages could be seen approaching him. The carter viewed him expectantly.

"Come from Wincanton, have you?"

"Yes. The market's busy today, you will be cheered to know. How much for a lot of apples?"

"'aypenny."

"I'll have one."

"Going far, are you?"

"To Bristol."

"Going to sea?"

"Never," said Sam.

"Free spirit, are you?"

"Exactly."

The carter smiled; Sam walked on, eating the apple. It was another thirty miles to Bristol. If the packet was due to leave in the early afternoon of tomorrow, he should be in very good time. The weather was still keeping fine. As he approached the next village, the trees formed a dark canopy around him, shadowing the path. Never before had he seen such deep green leafage. The village was not like that of Bourton. It seemed quaint, with cob-built thatched houses giving it a most ancient look. He was not fifteen miles from home, yet he was already in places unknown to him. Already he was a foreigner. A lad spoke out to him as he walked down the main road through the village; there was a slight unfamiliarity in his speech. I really have left home now, thought Sam. Within minutes he was out of the village again, continuing on along the westward road. He kept on walking, stopping here and there to eat, or to take the occasional alcoholic refreshment in the public-houses scattered sporadically along the way. He was two hours away from Bristol when night fell; he slept in a field some way off the roadside, under some trees, with his carpet-bag as a pillow and with only the rushing and retreating wind through the trees to distract him. He really was his own master now, he reflected, as he fell asleep in a joyful kind of exhaustion unknown to him before. He could do exactly as he wished. But he awoke before the sun was up and knew at once that the hour was five. Gratifyingly, he was soon asleep again and did not reawaken until well into the morning, unaware at first where he was and marvelling at his new surroundings.

It was with renewed vigour that Sam approached Bristol from the downward slope of a hill. The city appeared to be situated on an island, for it was partly surrounded by a river. He entered the city across a bridge; on either side stood two stone tollhouses each topped with a cupola. He got to the harbour, crowded with shipping; beyond lay the town and the tower. He walked along beside the warehouses, amongst drunks, merchants and sailor men until the red funnel of the steam packet came into view. The ship was a great iron vessel, with a flag at either end, each displaying name of 'SWIFT'. The day was still and calm, suitable for travel without undercover accommodation. Within the hour Sam was sitting and watching the horses and carriages being loaded on, trying not to burn his fingers on a hot potato bought from a stand. Eventually, they started taking on the passengers. When Sam finally got on board, he stood at the rail, staring out along the Usk; it seemed an age before the ship finally creaked and rumbled off, leaving the harbour and England behind. It was necessary to stand for the entire journey of two and a half hours. In rough weather it would have been three and a half, he was told by a member of the crew. As the land ahead became clearer and more visible, the sea became densely populated by other ships; the boat entered the mouth of a river that led into Wales, towards Newport, slowing down to a snail's pace. It finally seemed to be docking in at the left river bank, just before reaching an old stone bridge with arches, beyond which lay another bridge, made from timber and still under construction. The passengers were let off onto a stone stairway, which bent round, leading up to the road over the bridge and the street. He was standing in Wales. At once he headed for the stone bridge; on reaching it, he turned left into what appeared to be the High Street. It was wider than the High Street in Wincanton, with large stone buildings all along it, and filled with broughams, traps, and carriages. The ladies in hoop dresses were quite a cut above the women of Wincanton; he passed a group of gentlemen standing in the street, conversing, and was sworn at by a drunk beggar. Some of the inhabitants had dark hair worn over their shoulders in a way that he was not used to seeing. Sam had not drunk that day and was quite hungry and thirsty. He passed The Bridge Inn, but it was such a fancy place! The King's Head Hotel was equally daunting. But a little way on as the street bent round was an inn called the Tredegar Arms. It was situated next door to a strange looking old house with Tudor beams that seemed out of place in the modern town. The inn was open. He went in and ordered a beer and lunch. No one paid the least attention to him as he went in. Perhaps they thought he was local. But the bar maid seemed to recognise him as a stranger, for she asked him if he was just off the packet.

"Yes," said Sam. "How did you know?"

"Your travelling bag," said she. "They always end up here first, the young men who come from England. Not that we get that many."

"Do you know where I can get lodgings?" he asked her, on ordering his fare.

"Well, I don't know. Lodgings are scarce here, what with all the Irish, fleeing from the famine. What sort of lodgings do you want?"

"The cheapest. I'll sleep anywhere."

"Well, I should avoid the cheapest places, if I were you. Places like Fothergill Street and Charles Street, or anywhere where they are putting the Irish. There is no water there, and seven to a bed. The children sleep in the cupboards, so I've heard. The worst place of all is The Rookery, at the top of Stow Hill. Filth and vermin are rife there, and those that live there will rob you or attack you, or worse. Some go there, never to be seen again."

"Do you have rooms in this inn?"

"Yes. The tariff is one shilling and sixpence a night."

"Oh," said Sam.

"You could try the Dock-Parade," said the maid, help-fully. "There are clean rooms there, at not more than sixpence a night. Though you would still have to share, I should think. The room that is, not the bed."

"Share?" repeated Sam. Well, it will have to do, I suppose, he accepted. There was time for another two pints before he set off to find the accommodation. He contemplated a third, bringing his beer glass back to the counter but then changed his mind. "Where is Dock-Parade?" he enquired, anxiously.

The maid stepped out from behind the bar. Sam followed her to the doorway and outside. She pointed up the long High Street.

"Keep going in that direction and turn right at the end," she said.

Dock-Parade turned out to be alongside a newly built floating dock. The houses overlooking the dock were well built - it seemed quite a suitable place for a journeyman to lodge, as he should rightfully now be. The Dock Hotel stood at one end of the Parade, and he almost went in there, but on second thoughts went directly to the satisfactory accommodation of Miss Parfitt. The common room of the lodging-house was empty when he entered, which he took as a good sign; the apartment allocated to him was twice the size of that at home; the two beds that stood within were basic, but linen had been provided. Someone was already in the room. It was a young man about his own age, poorly dressed, who did not appear particularly interested to see him. "Good day to you," he said, hardly glancing at Sam then sitting down by the window on what he obviously regarded as his bed. Sam wondered where he was from and was about to ask when the man closed the faded curtains and fell back on the mattress, thereby reducing the chances of any communication to practically zero. Sam looked at him then decided to go out and explore more of the town. He went out of the room at once, taking his bag with him. Walking away from the Dock, he went up Commercial Road, down Commercial Street and into the High Street again.

There were a good many inns in Newport. Apart from The Tredegar Arms, there was also The Carpenter's Arms, a little further up; as there was also the Bunch of Grapes, which was actually a beer house. He went into this place. At a penny a pint, it was not long before he had got through half-a-shilling's worth. Finally emerging from this local, he headed off down the street again. He did not like to go into the larger inns, for he did not feel comfortable there, amongst the quality. Instead, he ambled into the side streets of the town, into further drinking establishments, such as the Ship and Castle, the Royal Oak and the Old Red Lion. No one was there to tell him otherwise, so he continued to drink all afternoon and evening. Time and duty were forgotten. He returned to his lodgings late at night when the house was in dark-ness and fell directly asleep, to be awoken by a stray dog barking. He brought out the watch from his pocket; it was half past eight. I have a year of sleep to catch up on, I think, he considered. The other man appeared to have already gone. How nice it is not to be working, his unashamed thoughts went on. I will have breakfast in town, and then I will see what I feel like doing. He rose, donning his usual clothes and taking his bag out with him again. The suit so generously donated by his mother remained wrapped up within it. It would not do to lose that. Perhaps he would need it some day.

How easy it was just to sit in public-houses and drink, with only a vague concern that his pockets were becoming lighter as each day passed. The beer always helped him to put the matter out of his mind. Only after three weeks, when he realised that he had but one shilling left in the world did he accurately re-evaluate the situation. The watch would have to go. Sitting in the Carpenter's Arms as he always did in the afternoon, he remembered having seen a pawnshop in Commercial Street. It would be desirable to proceed there directly. There was no question of him ever repaying a loan – an immediate sale would be the only acceptable possibility. He wondered how much he would get for the item.

As he walked down to the other end of the High Street, the familiar three golden balls of the pawnbroker were visible a hundred yards off. He quickened his pace and lost no time in entering the premises of Mr Leake, who appeared to be there in person, standing behind the counter.

"I wish to sell a watch," said Sam. "I will not be wanting it back."

"Let me see it." Mr Leake took the watch with the quaint design that Sam held out to him and examined it with the keenness of a hawk. He picked up a magnifying glass and turning the watch over, stared at it yet more intently. Sam waited patiently. Finally, the hard but honest looking man put the offering down upon the counter.

"I'll give you two pounds five shillings for it," he said, abruptly.

Sam had no idea how much it had cost in the first place. "That would be enough, I suppose," he said, gratefully.

Without any further ado, Mr Leake immediately opened the till with a cling, took the correct amount, handed it to Sam and shut the till again. All business was concluded. Feeling like a renewed and refreshed person, Sam went out into the street and headed back to The Carpenter's Arms. The thought of money now out of his mind, it seemed right to continue to drink and idle about. It would be some while before a need for money would arise again, and a further meeting with Mr Leake would become necessary. The days and nights continued with ease; but as the shillings and pennies disappeared from his pocket, insecurity set in once more. On a Friday morning, five weeks after arriving in Newport, he was down to his last shilling again. His mother's suit would have to be sold. But all Mr Leake could offer him this time was the lesser sum of one pound and five shillings.

As he lolled about in another inn at the end of Commercial Street, it seemed to him that it was now time to move on. Newport had shown him all that it could. I shall go farther up over the hills and see where that takes me, he decided. And no sooner had the decision been made than it was acted upon for he was out of Newport already by that afternoon, taking the northward road. In the fine spring climate, it would be no discomfort to tramp all day, sleeping in hedgerows. Several miles out he crossed a stone bridge thrown over the torrent of a grey river and ascended a steep hill whereupon he soon came up to a turnpike, where two roads from the south met. In the distance were whitened farmhouses scattered about, adding gaiety to the landscape. For certain they could be relied upon for food, in exchange for his few remaining shillings. He went on. Eventually, he came to immense mountains, abounding in steep and rough declivities, where he found it to be cold. A day later he came up to a place called Nant-y-glô, set among bleak and barren hills in a dreary, wild and almost uninhabited district. In front of him, a short distance away there appeared two round towers built from stone, lying at opposite corners of a great square wall. They had a medieval appearance, with slit windows and an iron door. They seemed to be there as a means of fortification, but exactly why fortification was needed in this day and age, he was not sure. Across a river were eight gigantic chimneys pouring out black smoke and a large, dull building that could well be an ironworks. Sam went over the bridge that led there. As he approached, he could hear the clanking and hammering of hard work and thought of retreating, but did not. When he got inside, it was an enormous, dark place, all on one floor, with a very high ceiling. Bright, glowing orange iron bars were being shifted around from furnaces to other machinery. Tired and hungry, Sam tried to find the foreman. Eventually, he was directed by a man cutting iron bars into short sections to a door at the far end of the factory. On it was a sign saying 'Clerk's Office.' Sam knocked and a moment later was called in.

Inside sat an unsympathetic looking official at a rough desk. A gentleman clad in a black cape and top hat stood beside him with a superior air. They were both looking critically at Sam, as he appeared before them, clearly asking for work.

"I am a fully apprenticed iron founder," said Sam, producing his certificate. "I come from Wincanton, in Somersetshire, where I served my time. I am only twenty-one years of age and could start work immediately."

The two potential employers continued to look un-enthusiastically at Sam.

"When did you last work?" asked the one at the desk.

"Not three weeks ago," said Sam. "It took me a while to get here."

"Are you always in that state?" asked the one in the cape, standing.

"You mean my clothes? These are my travelling clothes. I came straight here, as soon as I arrived in Nant-y-glô, in the hope of acquiring a position as soon as possible."

"There are no positions available. We do not take on those such as you," said the man at the desk, turning back to his work again. Sam left the office. As he hurried back through the hectic iron works, the sight of the men at their labour caused him to consider it no great tragedy to be rejected. A little later he was wandering along the village High Street where he found there to be even more public-houses than in Newport. As long as there were public-houses, he could live anywhere. He went into one and found beer to be cheaper there than in the cheapest inn in Newport. There, an aged man, clad in a red flannel shirt seemed to want to engage him in conversation. He seemed like a good person to ask about the round towers.

"The round towers? Oh, they've been there for thirty years," said the local. "They were built by Crawshay Bailey, owner of the ironworks. He needed them to protect himself and his family."

"What would he need to protect himself from?" asked Sam.

"From the workers," said the man, as though this were obvious. "He wouldn't pay the right wages, or reduce hours, so they rioted. After that Crawshay and his brother built a fortress, stocked with provisions, that they could run to should there be more aggravation. And there was."

"Does he live behind that wall?"

"No. The wall surrounds a farm complex. He lives on the other side of the complex, at Tŷ Mawr manor.

"Have you ever met him?"

"I've seen him once, a few years ago. Shortly before the last lot of riots, he came into the village, to investigate the trouble he was causing. Dressed in a long, black cape, he was, and lording it over everybody."

"I think I may have met him myself," said Sam. "I wouldn't want to meet him again."

"You probably won't," said the man. "I heard he's leaving the area very soon."

"I'm surprised he hasn't already if his life is at risk."

"Oh, it's not because he's afraid of us, I can tell you. He's decided to go into politics."

Sam finished his beer. Checking his money, he motioned for another.

"Looking for work here, are you?" asked the local.

"Yes," said Sam. "But I didn't get any."

"Just as well," said the man. "You won't find a harder taskmaster than Crawshay Bailey."

"I don't suppose you could tell me where I can find lodgings?" asked Sam. "I can't afford more than three pence a night."

"Three pence? You'll still get a roof above your head for that, I should think. I'm not familiar with lodgings. But they don't take kindly to strangers seeking work at low wages here. You better make it clear that you are just passing through."

"That I am," said Sam. "That I am."

*

On his last day in Nant-y-glô, Sam sold the boots off his feet to get food, his money and clothes now gone. If only he had never left his father's house! But it was too late now. Perhaps I could write home and explain what has happened, he thought for an instant but dismissed the idea as swiftly as it had come. He would have to continue as he had left off. The ground felt hard and stony beneath his bare feet as he started off in an easterly direction across an elevated tract of moor. When he reached the roadside, a milestone there was engraved XIX. to Monmouth. A day's walk, at least. Once out of the village a little way he saw a motherly sort of woman approaching him. As they were about to pass, he stopped her.

"Forgive me for troubling you," he began. "I am an iron founder who can not get employment. I am forced to travel the country against my own wish. I have no money for food."

The woman stared at him out of her unbelieving eyes. "I've got nout for you," she said finally and began walking off again. Sam quickened his pace slightly. In his hungry state, the sight of a local man coming up the road caused him to wonder if the codger was worth a penny.

"I am sorry to trouble you ..." he began again, as they met. "I am desperately hungry. I am an iron founder who is seeking employment."

"I'll give you a bit of bara caws," said the man, getting some bread and cheese out of his pocket. "Oh, I am most grateful," said Sam. And grateful he was. But it seemed like it was going to be difficult to get money out of the Welsh. Passing through more mountainous regions, he begged for money but got only food. It would seem he

44

could have a bagful if he so wished. As he went on, he wondered why he had seen no Welsh tramps.

By twilight, he reached a place of grassland and fruit trees, diversified by hill and dale, with a church and cottages. From here he could see the town of Monmouth, standing low in the wooded hills beyond. It could be no more than six or seven miles away. It was to the union in Monmouth to which he was heading; there had to be a workhouse there, for Monmouth was undoubtedly as large as Newport, and certainly as large as Wincanton, and both of these towns had workhouses. If I can be there after ten there will be no question of any work required of me at that late hour, he thought. And I believe that every workhouse is obliged to give out free bread and cheese on arrival.

The streets of Monmouth were well-laid out and lit with gas. When he found the building, it was obviously the right place; it had the size and grandness of a manor, yet there was something austere about it, suggesting that it was purpose built. Sam breezed up to the front entrance doors. He was about to pull on the bell when the doors were suddenly opened, and a harsh-looking official with a candle admitted him into the waiting hall. He was lead to a little window that looked into a kind of porter's lodge, into which the man went. The man got out a huge ledger book and placed it open on the counter.

"What is your name?" he enquired.

"Sam Brazenall."

"Your age?"

"Twenty-one."

"Your trade?"

"Iron founder."

"And where did you sleep last night?"

"In lodgings in Nant-y-glô."

"Travelling to find work, are you?"

"Yes, that's right."

"You can go in the tramp's room." The man shut the book again. Then he went over to an oversized breadbasket filled with square cut chunks of bread, took one, then took a piece of cheese from a cupboard beside the breadbasket, and unceremoniously presented Sam with the two free articles. Sam smiled. "Thank you most kindly, Sir," he said. He began to eat immediately.

"Here's a blanket," said the official, thrusting a cover that looked more like a rug through the window. The man re-emerged from the lodge and locked it. "This way," he said, walking away down a corridor that led off from the waiting hall. At the end of it was a long, narrow room. "Your bunk's at the end," said the man, leaving Sam to grope his way in the dark, amongst the stench of inmates, between the rows of bunks that were all lined up against the wall on either side. He found the empty bunk; it was just a bare plank, supported on either side by a wooden partition, separating him from the next bunk. Crouching down, Sam got into it and tried to lie down. It was really hard and uncomfortable. Surely the beds could have been better than this. How would he get any sleep at all in this kind of place? He no longer had his carpet bag to use as a pillow. He pulled the rug over himself and shut his eyes, but his tired state did not result in slumber. The bedroom in By-The-Way Cottage shared with Daniel was the utmost luxury, he now realized. But I can never expect shelter under my father's roof again, that I know, he continued to think. My father will never take me in if

I go back; otherwise, I would go back tomorrow. I must pluck up my spirits and forget where I am – that is the only way now. There is but one place for someone in my situation to go – the streets of London. There walk the rich and famous, loaded with excess money ready to fall into the hands of the eager beggar. There must be many who live off the wealthy in London. If I cannot survive there, I cannot survive anywhere. Yes, there I must go. With this thought, he finally managed to half-sleep until dawn, when he was rudely awakened by the ringing of a bell and light shafting into the long, narrow room. He could now see all those present; as they came into motion, he could not help but notice how extraordinarily grimy they were. Never before had he seen clothes so black and shiny with grease, and so worn and faded. He thought he was about to be led off to a dining hall where a breakfast awaited him, followed by work, but instead he was abruptly directed back to the little office with the wicket window again. Another lump of bread and piece of cheese were thrust before him.

"You're to leave at once," said the official. "We don't want your type in here any longer than necessary." Sam left the premises of the workhouse without any argument. A safe distance away, he sat beside the London Road, eating the second lot of bread and cheese that the Government of England had donated to him. Looking back along the road, he saw what looked like a common, vulgar sort of girl approaching him, who had apparently also spent the night at the union. As she came up closer, he could see that she wanted to speak to him.

"Are you on your way to London?" she enquired of him, demandingly.

"I am," said Sam.

"Can I walk alongside you?"

"It's a free country." Sam continued to chomp away at his food. The girl sat down next to him.

"Are you on the tramp?" Her voice was insistent.

"I suppose so," said Sam. "Though I never intended it that way."

"Things will be better in London," said the girl. "I have been there many times."

"It has to be better than here," said Sam.

The girl sat down beside him. He ignored her, eating faster now. But when Sam stood up again to start off along the road to London, she continued to tag along. "How long have you been tramping?" she was now asking.

"Oh, only a day or two. I've no money, you know."

"Oh, I didn't think you would have. But I don't want money. That's not why I wanted to walk with you. It's your company I want. Someone to be on the road with. I can be very alone on the road. Not to mention the dangers that a woman might meet with on the way – if you know what I mean ..." Sam was no longer listening. The next workhouse was more than likely not for another twenty miles. He planned on doing no more than eleven miles per day. In the month of May, there would be little difficulty in sleeping in the wild. Winter was an eternity away. May was bright with promise – yet he did not feel like one who was promised.

"We'll be better off in the lodging-houses than the workhouses." He became aware that the woman was speaking again. "They will separate us in the workhouses."

"I know," said Sam. "I think we're better off that way."

"Oh? Well, suit yourself. But I know this road well. I can tell you which of the big houses to stop off at."

"Can you."

"I can get you so much broken victuals at the right houses that you will be puzzled how to carry the load. You might as well bury me later than as now."

"What sort of houses are the right houses?"

"The mansions, out in the country. The villas just outside town are never any good. All you'll get is women shaking their fingers at you and servants slamming doors in your face."

I suppose I could put up with her for a little longer, thought Sam. The thought of knocking on the doors of strangers and standing alone on their doorsteps was not entirely appealing.

"I can see I shall have to rely on you," said Sam. "Until we get to London, that is. There I intend to conduct my own affairs."

"And I too," said the girl. "I have many acquaintances there, amongst the … shall we say, the more enterprising members of society."

"Please do not introduce me to them," said Sam. "They sound like the wrong sort of people to me."

"Quite fancy yourself, don't you? Well, you won't for much longer. You are going to need at least threepence a night for lodgings in London, and there aren't many ways to get it. You'll soon come down off your high horse, I can tell you."

"Please could you not talk so much," snapped Sam. "I can't stand a woman who goes on."

"All right, all right, I won't say a word unless I have to." She seemed not in the least bit tired. "They gave me a mattress in the union because I told them I was expecting," she added.

"How far is it to the next union?" asked Sam.

"Twenty miles. We can get there by this evening. Or we can do it in two stages. Normally I tramp ten miles a day."

Tramping is a way of life, observed Sam. It was already coming naturally to him. He began to imagine what London would be like; surely it could not be dull. In any case, there would be drink there, as there was anywhere else, at a price that even a beggar could afford.

"Have you stayed at any of the London workhouses?" he asked her, as they continued to trudge.

"Oh, yes. But I prefer the lodging-houses. They don't push you around there. You can do as you like."

"But you have to pay threepence."

"Oh, I'll soon get that, don't you worry."

"I'm sure you will," said Sam. I will spend no more time than is necessary with this woman, he decided, as if he had not already. As soon as we get to London, I shall be rid of this woman at the first opportunity. Perhaps she is of use now, but in London, she will be a burden. In a big city, I can travel much faster alone. It will not be a stone's throw from one workhouse to the next. It will take me at least a week to tour them. I just hope there will not be work to be done. I believe that there was stone-breaking to be done in the workhouse at Wincanton.

CHAPTER 4

The day after arriving in London, Sam disappeared from the view of the girl. This had not been difficult, for on their arrival in London, she had taken him to a lodging-house in the East End where they had entered an incredibly smoky kitchen. So thick was the fog in the room that you could barely make out those inside; a smell of herring and a glow at one end indicated that some of them were cooking their dinners. The others appeared to be lolling around on the floor or sitting on benches all around the side of the room. He had slipped out again at the first opportune moment, back into a large open yard and into a narrow court. Then without even looking back, he had run on into the street beyond, past a lot of Jew shops and public-houses where ragged children ran about, and women stood around, capless and bonnetless. He had continued to hurry on until he came up to Whitechapel and its union, but there they had said they were already full up. So on he had walked, through the gas-lit streets of London for miles and miles in the dark, wondering how it was that the air in London could be so putrid. Finally he had arrived at Marylebone Workhouse where he had been admitted; that was twelve hours previously. Now, standing somewhere along the New Road, in the vicinity of St Pancras, he was vaguely aware that it was Wednesday morning. He was beginning to feel a little weak; the crust of bread donated by the Marylebone Workhouse was long gone. He reached a spot where he felt he could begin his new occupation. From his only remaining pocket, he drew out the piece of chalk that he had earlier procured. Thereupon, in a fine, scholastic hand, he traced out the words, 'I am starving'. His work having been done, he sat languidly back against the wall of the street building. He had the whole day ahead of him.

It was as though he did not exist. His view of the pedestrians was confined to their lowermost parts; carriage wheels rumbled past continuously in the road beyond. The sun was beating down; he preferred to wear his hat rather than use it as a coin box. One man disdainfully altered the direction of his walk as he came nearer, and a woman pulled her child away from 'that worthless tramp who is probably diseased'. His monotonous, embarrassing existence continued mercilessly until without warning, he heard the sudden chink of a coin falling against the pavement. He looked up, but the perpetrator had already disappeared amongst the throng.

It was a silver shilling. How long would it have taken him to earn as much in the iron foundry? Several hours on apprentice wages, that was for sure. He hurriedly put it away into his pocket. How long had he been sitting there? It was hard to say, but surely no longer than twenty minutes. However, one swallow did not a summer make, as he had repeatedly inscribed in his long-lost calligraphy classes at the school in Wincanton. He continued to sit with his head lowered. When he looked up again, he thought he could see a policeman observing him from the other side of the street. He got up immediately and walked quickly away.

A safe distance along the road he went directly into a public-house by the name of The Adam and Eve. It was as crowded as the thoroughfare without, with nowhere to sit; Sam took himself through the lunchtime throng of artisans into a back parlour where everything was mahogany; the chairs were mahogany, the benches were mahogany, the walls were dark panelling. All the customers within were seated. In the corner at the back, he could see a young lady with an attitude of quiet confidence, listening steadily to a man dressed in an expensive-looking suit, with his back to Sam. They looked somewhat out of place. There was a space on a bench near the door. Sam sat down. The woman did not appear to notice him, so engaged was she in her companion's conversation. Perhaps it is just as well, thought Sam, considering my ragged, dirty appearance. But there is another life, of that I am now sure. That woman is the real life.

He continued to look incessantly at the woman. Finally, the two appeared to be leaving. She and the man walked out through the discreet side door, still with no apparent notice of his presence. The man was without a doubt affluent; I now know there is more to money than just materialistic comfort, he decided; money is of importance where women are concerned, it would seem. And at this moment, I have none at all.

"What is your pleasure?"

There was now a barmaid standing at the table. "Oh, whatever you have for a shilling, if you please," said Sam, "including a pint of ale." His gaze was still fixed on the empty table at the back. It remained empty for the next fifteen minutes until the dinner plate arrived. Sam gobbled down the food. It was the first decent meal he had had for three days.

I suppose I had better be getting back to work, he thought, finally. And I had better find another spot. One that is free of roaming policemen. He stepped out into the street again and walked on all the way to King's Cross, whereupon he took the road leading off to the right, towards the city. He found a street that already appeared to be inhabited by several famished beggars. Perhaps it would be better not to interfere with their business. He moved hurriedly away, ever closer to the epicentre of London. Eventually, he found a long, new street that began near the abbey, so new that it was still in the process of being built, where a spot halfway along seemed appropriate for his purposes. Not a beggar in sight was there. He sat down, chalking out again the same three words that were expected to generate his income. But hardly were they written, when an officer of the law appeared from nowhere. "Get up, son," he was saying. "You must come along with me." Sam got to his feet. With a whirling head, he was dragged by the arm across the road, along a side street, hardly noticing the shocked glances from passing pedestrians until they reached a police station. Here he was forcibly ushered into a back parlour, where the police officer informed the sergeant on duty of the charge on which Sam had been arrested. It was duly written down. Sam was not required to say anything and so did not speak. The next time that he saw the police officer the man was standing in the witness box, repeating to the magistrates the course of events. His slow and earnest words were written down by the clerk and magistrate alike. Two other witnesses were also called whom Sam did not recognize; one woman said she had often seen him begging on the streets of London, while another said that she believed him to be the one guilty of pick-pocketing in the New Road the day before. However, they could not substantiate their suppositions. When Sam's turn came, he could not defend himself. Yes, he had sat down in Victoria Street, and yes, he had written in chalk on the pavement. No, he was not exactly sure what constituted begging, but he would refrain from repeating his actions.

Then he was aware that the judge himself was addressing him. The last bit was that he was to be given the lamentably lenient sentence of seven days confinement within the premises of Westminster Bridewell.

Westminster Bridewell was surely a forbidding place when seen from the outside. A great wall the height of several men surrounded it. In a central position was the stone arch gateway, with the carved key within.

This is exactly like the workhouse, thought Sam, as he was conducted into the reception room by the official of the lodge; here they were handed over to a clerk. The old, familiar routine began again.

"What is the prisoner's name, age, number of times previously convicted, etc." He was soon donning an iron grey suit, after which he was marched off to a small cell and presented with a bowl of gruel. But no sooner had he consumed this, and it had taken him less than a minute to do so, he was ordered out of his cell, to march with a gang of men, five feet apart, to a long room with walking galleries high up all along the walls, below which a gigantic drum with steps was rotating, driven by prisoners, each of whom were separated on either side by a partition, so that he could neither see nor speak to anyone. Sam was ordered to sit down on the bench at one side of the room. From there he could see officials walking up and down the galleries, observing any deviations from the required action, such as a man stepping off the wheel or attempting to communicate with another prisoner. After about five minutes, the men all got off the drum, and he was told to get up and walk to the wheel.

Within his allotted partition was a chain with a handle on the end. Sam grabbed hold of this and stepped onto the wheel. Putting all his weight upon the steps, it was hard to catch every one as it came round for they were not only close together but very small, allowing little more than room for the toes. At one minute, he missed one, and his foot slipped off painfully. The endless ladder continued on and on until the official called out 'time'. Sam got off and turned around. It was with a sigh that the men now sitting on the bench now had to get up to take his place. He went and sat back down, continuing to face ahead of him. At least the drink was coming out of him; when he got out, he would go to work again and be a sober man. Anything was better than continuing on like this. He thought of home, of his mother and how upset she would be to see him reduced to this. He thought of writing to her – would such a thing be allowed in this place? Most of the inmates could not write, more than likely. He would write the minute he got out; perhaps his mother could give him the money for some new clothes. She would send at least a sovereign, he was sure. With a sovereign, he could again find clothes, and with clothes, he could again find work. But before he knew it, he was walking back to the wheel again. As he trod for four hours upon the endless ladder, he considered it not so bad, but later a giddiness came over his eyes and hunger gnawed at his stomach. Again he thought work to be preferable to this and reminded himself repeatedly that as soon as he was out, he would devote himself to seeking employment.

In the morning he was given pencil and paper to write to his mother; the letter must have been the most convincing appeal to return to work that he had ever made but he did not mention that he was in prison. Perhaps the officials would do that for him.

When they let him out, and he was walking away from the prison in the open air, all thoughts of the treadwheel and the rope-picking suddenly left him; he was free to be back on the road again and to do as he liked. Food in workhouses was worse than prison, but he would only be staying the night. And so began his grand tour of England, visiting every workhouse on the way.

When winter came, and it began to snow, he headed back to London, where the asylums for the poor would now be open and would help to get him through the cold spell. The one he knew about was situated in Playhouse Yard; when he got there, the yard turned out to be a narrow lane. He found it to be full of gin palaces, oyster stalls and low-class pawnbrokers. At the time he was walking down this lane, early evening, it would be difficult to miss the asylum; for a throng of starved and tattered people extended along the way, leading up to a lamp which hung in a wire cage outside the establishment which was to house these individuals. They seemed even worse off than him; at least most of his garments still remained existent, although torn and worn in places. They all appeared as if they were not long in this world. Was he to become like these people? At the moment all he felt was cold.

"How long do we wait here for?" Sam asked the man in a short blue smock, standing just in front of him. The queue seemed to have been there for some time.

"Pardon, monsieur?" was his answer.

"That's French, is it not?"

"Oui, monsieur." And so the conversation continued. But the crowd was now oozing forwards.

When he got to the main gates, it was all much like the workhouses except that no work would be expected of him here. At the office window, he gave his name as Dick Turpin and occupation as carpet weaver. As the clerk wrote down rather slowly all his particulars, he observed a group of distinguished-looking visitors, standing at the back, spectating. Sam wondered what they were doing there. Finally he was handed his usual brick of bread, but as he walked away along the whitewashed corridor he overheard the clerk say, "We are obliged to let in such cases as those, for if we were to shut our doors because some impose upon us, we should be punishing the honest poor more than the dishonest." He took it in his stride. What would such people know about the poor, either honest or dishonest. He walked on upstairs to the tramp's ward, passing by the wash room and another little office window where more were queuing.

"What is this queue for?" enquired Sam of one of them.

"If you've been here before you need a ticket to come again."

"How long can you stay?"

"Three nights in a row, usually." The man began coughing. Everyone in the place seemed diseased, as though it were a hospital. Sam saw that the thermometer attached to a wooden pillar nearby was at forty-five degrees. Why could they not light the fires? It really was a bit cold for inside. But nobody seemed to be getting around to it. As Sam sat in his bunk up in the ward amongst the inmates, with their influenza and ague and inflamed lungs, the temperature continued to drop.

The following morning was ever more bitingly cold. Sam was standing in the tramp's ward together with a dozen others around the large double grate in the centre of the room. There now glowed a bright, piled-up coke fire, railed off all around. They had all been detained at the request of a journalist, who was to come that morning to interview those vagrants who for the price of a shilling, would give an account of their history. Not a word was said between them until someone incidentally intimated that it was a man's right to do anything rather than starve. This resulted in a gleam of merriment.

Finally, the awaited journalist arrived; an energetic man approaching forty, he walked straight into the ward in such a way as to suggest that everything in his life was fast and efficient. He was followed by a younger, dutiful assistant. Also accompanying them was the warden. The journalist's name was Henry Mayhew; his small claim to fame was that for the previous two years he had published articles on a weekly basis in the Morning Chronicle concerning the poorest in London. Two chairs had been provided for the visitors, beside a bench, upon which the subject would sit.

"If you could come one at a time," said Mr Mayhew. Sam came forward and was the first to be interviewed. The journalist Mr Mayhew sat on the chair directly in front of him. His side-kick was now holding a notepad and pencil and sat unobtrusively beside him.

"Now," began Mr Mayhew. "As I said, I am willing to give you a shilling for your story, but it must be truthful. Is this your first time in London?"

"No," said Sam. "I am known here, and if I tell you a lie now, you'll say, 'You spoke an untruth in one thing, and you'll do so in another.' It was last May that I first came to London, and I stopped until the 10th of June."

"Where do you come from and what is your trade?"

"I am from Wincanton in Somerset," said Sam. "I am a carpet weaver by trade. I served my time to it."

"And your family?"

"My father was a clerk in a flax mill in Bourton," revealed Sam. "He lived very comfortably; indeed, I was happy. Before I left home, I knew none of the cares of the world that I have known since I left. My father is still as well off as when I left home ...;" and so Sam continued on quite voluntarily, the journalist asking questions and the secretary making notes. "I am altogether tired of carrying on like this," he concluded. "I haven't made sixpence a day ever since I have been in London this time. I go tramping it across the country just to pass the time and see a little of new places. When the summer comes, I want to be off again. I am sure I have seen enough of this country now; and I should like to have a look at some foreign land. Old England has nothing new in it now for me."

"But you wish to remain a beggar," said the journalist, watching him all the time with an impartial expression.

"Oh, no," said Sam. "I think a beggar's life is the worst kind of life that a man can lead. There are too many at the trade. I wasn't brought up to a bad life. Indeed, I should like to have a chance at something else."

"How long have you been a vagabond?"

"Eight months," said Sam. "But I have had the feelings of a vagabond for a full ten years. But I know, and now I am sure, I'm getting to be a different man. I begin to have thoughts and ideas I never had before."

"How are you different?"

"Once I never feared or cared for anything," said Sam. "And I wouldn't have altered if I could, but now I'm tired out. Now I wish to go right. But if I haven't a chance of going right, why I must go wrong." He looked hopefully up at the journalist.

But Mr Mayhew did offer nothing but the promised shilling, which would soon be gone, leaving Sam in as sorry a state as before. His interview concluded, he ventured out into the frozen streets again, to find some place of warmth to spend the hours until nightfall, when he could and would return to the asylum.

On Thursday, 17th January, 1850, Mr Mayhew sat in a corner of the large, busy office of the Morning Chronicle in Fleet Street; he had before him the notes from the interviews at the asylums for the poor; from these he was now dictating to one of his army of assistants the article that was to appear the following day; this was simultaneously being written out again in longhand by another assistant. So far his contributions had been a major success, and he was well on the way to release from bankruptcy. He was in the middle of unbroken speech when his younger brother Augustus arrived on the scene.

"Henry. Sorry I'm late; I got held up this morning."

"Augustus, come and help me with this description," said Henry Mayhew. He picked up the piece of paper on which was hastily written the first page of the article. Augustus Mayhew took it and held it at arm's length.

"The first vagrant was one who had the thorough look of a 'professional'," he read out loud. "He was literally a mass of rags and filth. He was indeed, exactly what, in the act of Henry VIII, is denominated a 'valiant beggar'. His clothes, which were of fustian and corduroy, tied close to his body with pieces of string, were black and shiny from dirt, which looked more like pitch than grease. He had no shirt, as was plain from the fact that, where his clothes were torn, his bare skin was seen. You're getting almost as good as me," said Augustus cheerfully, putting down the paper.

"You can add nothing to it?"

"Well, let's see," said Augustus, picking up the paper again. "How about, 'His cap was an old, brimless 'wide-awake', and when on his head, gave the man a most unprepossessing appearance."

"An old, brimless 'wide-awake'? That's excessive, don't you think?"

"Well, it's a bit of colour."

"Very well. Put that in, could you?" he said, turning to the assistant. "Augustus, would you object to going out for lunch, now? I'm rather hungry. However, I must be back here in an hour."

"Not at all."

The brothers Mayhew stepped out of the offices of the Morning Chronicle and into Fleet Street. They strolled along the pavement packed with jostling, hurrying crowds, beside a roadway blocked up with cabs, omnibuses and vans. Although well accustomed to the dining rooms of The Strand, today Henry and his considerably younger brother would be content with a shilling snack, 'hot with vegetables,' at a nearby tavern. Very soon they stood at the counter of one of these overcrowded establishments brimming with clerks and City men. Henry spoke up above the noise, coming from both inside and out.

"Oh, Augustus, have you started the novel?"

"Yes. I have written a few passages based upon your impressive research. It may not become my best work, but its strength will be its extreme truthfulness. Your latest inquiries will give me marvellous descriptions of tramp-dom and vagrancy that I could never have formulated myself. And it should discourage those who will not work, for they will see the true nature of the life that is waiting for them, should they step off the straight and narrow. Thank you," said Augustus, as his half-steak was placed before him.

"Have you come up with a title?"

"Yes. 'The Romance and Reality of the London Streets.'"

"Too long. You need something short and snappy."

"Well, I am sure the publishers will change any title that I think of. Although one thing I shall insist upon is that underneath the title are written the words, 'An unfashionable novel.' The book is to be based on reality, not fantasy."

"I am sure it will be successful."

"In view of your meticulous research, it deserves to be. And if your articles are anything to reckon by, it should be of great interest to the upper and middle classes. They delight in romanticising the plight of the poor."

"And do nothing to aid it."

"But you have made them aware of it. That is the purpose of the journalist. And who knows who will read your reports."

At 4.26 p.m. on Friday, 18 January, 1850, a part-time city worker by the name of Mr Davenport was at his club in St James' Street, London. He was the only member there that afternoon. He was seated in a green leather armchair, near the fire, casually reading a copy of The Morning Chronicle. The article which had caught his eye was one describing the most unfortunate members of society with no fixed address and no visible means of support, who were forced to move around from one union workhouse to the next, begging and stealing. But why were they so unfortunate? He could not imagine himself ever ending up in such a situation.

He was awaiting the arrival of another member, who should turn up at any minute. This man rarely frequented the club, for he was a country member. As the man in question walked through the doors of the club, Mr Davenport got out of his chair to greet him.

"I hope you haven't had to sit here waiting for me for too long," the man from the country began.

"No, not at all." They sat down together again. A waiter

appeared and enquired what he would like to drink. The man ordered a whisky and soda.

"Anything for you, Sir?"

"Oh, I'll have another whisky and soda, as well, if you please." The waiter went away.

"It's certainly very quiet in here, today," commented the man from the country.

"Yes, it is, rather," said Mr Davenport. "Practically no one else has been in here. I've spent the last half an hour reading the Morning Chronicle. Actually, there's a very interesting article in there today. It concerns the vagrant population of Britain. I had no idea there were so many of them. Overrunning our country, they seem to be. It seems to be the fault of those union workhouses that have been stationed in practically every town. They are effectively free hotels for the non-working population."

"Not a hotel that I would wish to stay at."

"Oh, the vagabond has little or no concern for his sur-roundings. He will sleep anywhere."

"Well, such free hostelries must not be closed," objected the country member. "For there are those who are actively and genuinely seeking work and must travel to find it. To refuse asylum to the vagrant is to shut out the traveller – so hard is it to tell the one from the other."

"So you would allow vagrancy to prevail."

The other member paused to think.

"I do not regard it as desirable," he said, finally. "However I do believe it to be curable. The prime cause of vagrancy may be the non-inculcation of the habit of industry. Labour and effort are more or less irksome to us all. But once the habit of working is formed, labour can be rendered easy."

"I do not believe a want of habit to be the primary cause of vagrancy," objected Mr Davenport. "Many of the vagrants mentioned in this article come from respectable backgrounds and were practising trades before they chose to break away. Thus they were in the habit of working and wished to escape from it."

"Well, perhaps habit is not the only thing that might encourage a vagrant to work," amended his friend. "The excitement of some impulse or purpose would also have such an effect. The vagrant has no such purpose."

"They do have a purpose. Their purpose is to wander. It is their only natural inclination," returned Mr Davenport.

"You cannot deny that they are in a state of destitution; unable to find work, they are driven to vagrancy for it is the only way of existence open to them."

"Again, I am afraid I disagree. The prime cause of vagrancy is not a non-inculcation of the habit of industry, nor is it a lack of purpose, nor in fact, is it the pressure of a state of unavoidable want or destitution; it arises from the temptation of obtaining property without regular industry."

"Getting something for nothing, in other words."

"Exactly so. They have the mentality of the gamblers at the card tables in this club."

"Well, if these vagrants were, in fact, gentlemen, and chose to live their lives in idleness, rather than being despised they would be greatly respected. The vagrant touring the workhouses of England is not unlike the gentleman on his Grand Tour of Europe."

"You are quite right." Mr Davenport picked up the newspaper again. "One of the vagrants in this article says that when the summer comes, he wants to be off to some foreign land; as though he were some kind of aristocrat. The impudence of it. The only foreign land he'll ever see is Van Diemen's land."

"Perhaps a more sympathetic approach to the vagrant's lot would be helpful," said the country member. "Criticism serves only to make them yet more obstinate. They deserve a second chance."

"You have too much sympathy, Bewley," said Mr Davenport. "Sympathy for women, sympathy for animals and now sympathy for vagrants. They will only take advantage of you."

"Well, why not let them demonstrate that they deserve your sympathy? Before being given employment, they must show that they are willing to do a job with more effort than is actually needed for it. To do this, they will be given some form of work that could be done efficiently, but which they will be required to do tediously. An example of which could be, the cleaning of a floor with the aid of only a toothbrush. This will distinguish those who have the desire to work from those who do not."

"None of these vagrants will do a task with any more effort than is required of it. As I said, and as you so neatly rephrased it, they prefer to go the other way and get something for nothing. If given a toothbrush to clean a floor, they will use a scrubbing brush. Or they will find someone else to do it."

"And I am of the opinion that they will do the task as directed. As a vagrant, they are free, but the price of freedom has been bought only at the cost of a very hard life. They want no more of it."

Mr Davenport folded the newspaper. "Well, we can

soon sort out this matter," he said, standing up. "We will go round to the asylum and bring out a couple of them. They will be set to work in my garden, under the supervision of my gardener. He will give them some work to be done in the nature that you describe. I'll wager a hundred sovereigns to ten that they will not complete it."

"I accept."

"In the unlikely event that they do the task as instructed, I will consider finding them further employment."

"Nothing could be fairer."

"My wife was hoping you could come round for dinner tomorrow evening."

"I would be quite happy to accept."

"If I set the vagrants to work during the day, we should have the results when you arrive."

"That sounds capital. Your wife is aware, I hope, of my vegetarian requirements."

"No, but I shall inform her. Well, shall we go? The newspaper informs me that the asylum is situated in a lane off Whitecross Street, in Cripplegate."

"I will allow you to lead the way. Do not let us remain there any longer than necessary – I do not wish to succumb to any sub-tropical diseases, if at all possible."

"You are right, Bewley. I appreciate your concern. A visit to the poor quarters of London is not unlike going on a safari, and similar precautions must be taken. If you wish, you can wait for me at the top of Aldersgate, and I shall proceed to the asylum alone."

"No, I will come with you," said Bewley, getting up.

The attentive waiter stared dubiously after the two gentlemen as they left the club room, wondering if he would ever see them again. He was not in a hurry to visit

68

those slums which he had once called home and to which the gentlemen were now heading. It seemed unheard of that men of their class would even think of going to such a place. As he picked up the two empty glasses, he caught a glance of the newspaper article which had interested them so greatly and reflected that the world must be changing.

CHAPTER 5

The not inconsiderable residence of Mr Davenport, of Wellington Road, St John's Wood, London, N.W. was surrounded by a walled garden, front and back. During the spring and summer months it seemed to require constant attention, but in the winter there was little to do. Mr Davenport had left for the city that morning, after giving his gardener strict instructions concerning two vagrants that he had collected from an asylum for the poor; they were to be given a good breakfast, after which they were to be set to work immediately in a manner that he would then describe. Although on hearing the plan he had not been wholly in accordance with it, the gardener had nodded and Mr Davenport had stepped out of the great gate at the front of the house. Now, one hour later, Sam and his companion juvenile were sitting in the outhouse at one side of the back garden, awaiting directions.

"This truss of hay," said Mr Greengage, indicating the tied-up bale at one end of the outhouse, "is to be transported to the other outhouse over there, see?" He pointed to this second location on the west side of the house. "That may sound like easy work, but the master wants it done one straw at a time." He untied the truss. "Any other way isn't allowed. Is that understood?"

The two juveniles nodded.

"Well, in that case, I'll leave you to it." Mr Greengage stomped off towards the house. Sam's companion immediately sat down on the truss.

"Quite a fancy house, is it not?" he observed, with a leer.

"Yes," said Sam. "I'm not getting involved in anything, though."

"I don't know what we're going to do all day."

"You heard what he said. One straw at a time."

"No, we'll just carry it over in a couple of loads at the end of the day."

Sam disentangled one of the straws and went out into the freezing air. As he walked across the frozen ground of the garden, a robin hopped out of the trees before him; perhaps a bird could do the job faster. When he reached the second outhouse, he opened the shut door and placed it on the stone floor inside. Then he crossed over the garden again, thinking what a cold time he would have of it, crossing continuously. He glanced towards the generously built house; Greengage appeared to be watching him from the kitchen window.

Back in the first outhouse, he pulled out another straw.

"Is this your idea of having fun?" asked the other.

"We're being observed," said Sam. "From the house."

"So?"

"So, this is obviously some kind of test."

"Well, as long as we transport the stuff, we're going to get paid anyway, I know it. You're wasting your time."

Sam walked out and across again, this time a little faster. He was sure that he was still under examination from Greengage, although the man was no longer visible.

If he carried on, employment was in sight; though he had to admit what he was doing at the moment was hardly work for a grown man. Back in the first outhouse again, the other was refusing to shift from his comfortable position. Crossing his legs, he observed Sam with less respect than might be expected.

"You're looking pretty silly, did you know?"

"Yes," said Sam, picking up another straw. "I hope you're warm in here."

"Oh, I'm most comfortable," said he, pulling his feet up onto the truss of hay. Sam went out again.

At this moment Mrs Davenport was taking tea in the blue room at the back of the villa overlooking the garden. Her husband was not at home, so she had at that moment only the servants for company. The parlour-maid had just left the room; the mistress had conversed with her in a polite and friendly fashion about how well the new housemaid was settling in, and the pattern on the curtains that the parlour-maid had sewn for their attic room. But now she was alone again. Taking a sip of the laboriously prepared Lapsang Souchong tea, she gazed dreamily out of the window. Sam was at this moment crossing the garden for about the fifteenth time. The sight of this ragged man walking barefoot over the hardened snow, carrying what appeared to be a straw, struck her as very strange. She stood up gracefully from the divan and walked over to the window, carrying the cup and saucer. The man disappeared into one of the outhouses, only to re-emerge seconds later and to cross over the garden again, without the straw. On reaching the other outhouse, he went in and soon came back out again, with another straw.

Mrs Davenport glided over to the bell-pull in one corner of the elegant room. She tugged it decisively, then glided back over to the divan, sitting down as gracefully as she rose. Presently, Greengage entered the room.

"Greengage, who on earth is that man outside in the garden and what on earth is he doing?" she enquired, at once.

"Oh, that's one of your husband's vagrants, Madam. He picked two up from the Asylum for the Houseless last night, told them to come round this morning. They've had a good breakfast in the kitchen, and now we've set them to work."

"What work are they doing?"

"They're transporting hay, Madam. From one out-house to the other. It don't really need to be done, it's just a sort of trial. To see if they've got hard work in them, you see, Madam."

"One of my husband's ridiculous experiments."

"Yes, Madam. I'm assigned to be watching them. Though only one of them's come out of the outhouse, the other's just sitting in there, waiting for the day to end."

"Well, this has just got to stop, immediately. Dismiss the one in the outhouse and send the other to me, will you, Greengage?"

"Yes, Madam. Wouldn't he be too dirty for in here, Madam?"

"Well, put some newspaper on that chair over there. He can sit on that."

"Yes, Madam." Greengage took the newspaper from the coffee table and placed several large sheets over the velvet upholstery of the elegantly carved wooden chair nearby. He then left the room without more ado.

A few minutes later, Greengage entered the room again, followed by a bewildered-looking young fellow; the vagrant had removed what remained of his hat from his head and clutched it before him, as though protecting himself.

"Sit down," commanded Mrs Davenport, imperiously indicating the newspaper-covered chair.

Sam sat down. He had vaguely recovered himself now. He wondered if Mrs Davenport was going to offer him some tea. His throat was parched.

"Thank you, Greengage," said Mrs Davenport. Greengage went immediately.

"What is your name?" began Mrs Davenport.

"Sam Brazenall."

"You are not a servant here, so I shall not ask you to call me Madam. Well, Sam, Greengage tells me that you are a vagrant seeking employment."

"Yes, Madam."

"What is your trade?"

"I am an iron founder," said Sam, sadly. "At least, I was."

"Why did you leave your employment?"

Sam shifted uncomfortably.

"Well, I was coming towards the end of my apprenticeship and decided to take a little time off work. At first it was grand. But then things went bad; as you can see from my state, it all ended like this." He stared miserably at the Persian rug on the floor.

"How long have you been a vagrant?" asked Mrs Davenport, kindly.

"Eight months, Madam. More like eight and a half.

I'll do anything to escape this life. I'm no more thought upon than a dog in the street."

"Have you not attempted to find employment during this time?"

"Yes, Madam. But they won't even look at me, dressed as I am."

"Have you really no other clothes?"

"No, Madam."

"But you're dressed in rags. That jacket is almost about to fall apart altogether. And as for tying up the sleeves with bits of string ... it's quite unbelievable."

Sam could only agree.

"Have you been wandering around all winter dressed like that?"

"Yes, Madam."

"I'm surprised you haven't caught your death of cold," said Mrs Davenport. "And you look half-starved. Did they not give you food and clothing at the asylum?"

"Just a piece of bread, Madam. No clothes. I've been wearing these clothes for eight months."

"Well, this is terrible," said Mrs Davenport, clearly meaning it. "The asylums are obviously not what they should be."

"No, Madam."

Perhaps I should join one of our do-good committees, thought Mrs Davenport. It may be that my help is needed after all. "I had no idea that such conditions of poverty existed," she said. "Or I should most certainly have done something for those wretched members of our society."

"Oh, it can get a lot worse than this, Madam. Down in the Flower and Dean Street Rookery. If you could only see the filth and vermin there ..."

"Perhaps I should visit the rookeries," said Mrs Davenport. "To see them for myself."

"Well, if you'll take my advice, you won't go down there," said Sam. "There's the pox, and the scarlet fever, both rife in those parts. You would not last a fortnight."

"Yes, maybe you are right," said Mrs Davenport, rapidly coming to her senses. "But I am convinced that something must be done. To think that a man like you should be reduced to living under such conditions."

"Well, it's my own fault, Madam," said Sam. "When I left my apprenticeship, I longed just to drink and idle about. I loved a roving, idle life. I much preferred to be on the road than at home. But now I am a different man."

"Have you ever been in prison?"

"Yes. Once. But only for fourteen days."

"What were you imprisoned for?"

"Begging and vagrancy. I never stole."

"You have never stolen to keep yourself alive?"

"Only apples from barrows, Madam. Everybody does that. Everybody on the streets that is."

"Yes, I am sure that they do. Have you no desire at all to work?"

Sam lowered his head. "Well, actually, Madam, there was one placement that at one time did attract me. As a child, I wanted desperately to be a mail guard."

"A mail guard?" Her tone was as Sam expected.

"Yes, Madam. It seemed exciting and glamorous to me, like being a highway man, only in reverse. But I would never know how to go about getting such a position."

"You would wish to be out in the cold, fifteen hours at a time, in all weathers, with no opportunity to enter an inn at intervals, as would the driver and his passengers?"

76

Sam looked up and said nothing.

"A mail guard's duty is to guard the mail bag. And that he would do, remaining on the outside of the coach at all times. In mid-winter, such an ordeal would not bear thinking about."

"Perhaps you are right," said Sam. "As I said, it was only a childhood fantasy. I have put away childish things now."

"In any case, I would not have the means to procure you such a position, even if I wished to. Mail guards usually have had a former position of the nature of footman, or cabdriver, or some suchlike. But I am sure there will be something I can do for you – I cannot let you leave here in your sorry state. You are presentable and receptive, and I have sufficient faith in you to provide you with employment in my own home, at least, on a trial basis. Would that be acceptable to you?"

"Anything would be acceptable to me," said Sam, sitting upright in the chair. "I have reached the bottom rung of the ladder."

"Then it is settled," said Mrs Davenport, rising again from the sofa and walking over to the bell-pull. "Greengage and Mrs Renshaw my cook will prepare you for your duties. We have a visitor to dinner this evening, so your services will be most timely. We shall be able to dine à la Russe."

"Thank you, Madam," said Sam, standing up. "I am most grateful."

"I quite believe that you are," said Mrs Davenport, sitting down again. Sam continued to stand. There was a pause, mercifully broken by the entrance of Greengage. Sam observed how the man stared at his mistress in disapproving expectation.

"I have decided to engage this young man as footman," said Mrs Davenport. "Please take him downstairs and sort him out. He is to wait at table tonight."

"Oh, I don't know if we can get him ready by then, Madam," said Greengage.

"Well, try," said Mrs Davenport.

"Yes, Madam." Greengage turned casually towards Sam, who followed him directly out of the room.

Mrs Davenport glanced listlessly at the tea things on the coffee table; beside them lay a copy of *The World of Fashion*. She picked it up and turned the pages slowly and disinterestedly. It must have been about half-past nine, or a quarter to ten. Her husband would not be home until four o'clock, accompanied by his companion. It would be some time until then. It occurred to her to go downstairs to the kitchen to see how they were getting on with the vagrant; but then she decided that it might not be entirely appropriate for her to do so.

She turned to look out of the windows again. Greengage was in the garden. He appeared to be pinning some bare fruit tree branches to the back wall. Spring would be early this year, he had told her. Everything would be better in the spring, she was sure.

CHAPTER 6

At five o'clock that evening, Mr Bewley from the county of Buckinghamshire was sitting in the gas-lit dining room of the private residence of his host, Mr Davenport. The relaxing environment was most agreeable to him.

"I hope you like the vegetarian rissoles," said Mrs Davenport, anxiously. "I'm afraid we really didn't know what to provide for you."

"They are capital," said Mr Bewley. "Never before have I been so well received."

The door opened and Sam walked in, dressed in full footman wear. The transformation in his appearance was incredible. His face, previously covered in grease and grime, was now washed and shaven. His hair, now several shades lighter, was cut and combed. He walked discreetly over to the sideboard at the back of the room and stood there quietly and unobtrusively, as he had been instructed to do. However, he appeared to have aroused the attention of the table.

"I say, don't I know you?" asked Mr Bewley, abruptly. "You seem damned familiar."

Sam looked towards his addresser and immediately recognised him as being the philanthropist, who, accompanied by another gentleman, had picked him up from the asylum the evening before. The other gentleman now appeared to be sitting at the far end of the table.

"Yes, Sir," he said, very politely. "I believe we met yesterday, at the Asylum for the Houseless Poor."

"Good Heavens. It can't be … yes, it is you, I'm sure of it. Well, you've certainly moved up in the world since I saw you last."

"Yes, Sir."

"What's going on, Bewley?" asked the other gentleman, whom Sam now assumed to be Mrs Davenport's husband.

"He's one of those vagrants we collected from the asylum last night. Do you not recognise him? And why is he now a footman in your house?"

Mr Davenport stared confusedly at Sam. "I really don't know," he said.

"I have engaged him," explained Mrs Davenport, calmly.

Mr Davenport continued to look towards Sam, then at his wife.

"Was that really a good idea, Cordelia?" he asked.

"Well, you are always telling me to experiment. I am merely continuing the experiment that you initiated by bringing him in here in the first place."

"Yes, but to put a man to casual work in the garden is one thing. To appoint him to an important household position without a character is another. In any case, I thought we had agreed that we did not need a footman."

"Mrs Fortescue has a footman," argued his wife. "And her home is no larger than ours."

"I consider that to be completely irrelevant," said Mr Davenport.

"Well, the experiment worked far better than I

expected," interjected Mr Bewley. "Never in my wildest imaginings did I expect to be waited on this evening by one of the sad, hopeless figures that we sought out yesterday. He has risen from vagrant to footman in less than twenty-four hours. It just shows what is possible when there is a will."

"Bewley, I have not forgotten about your a hundred sovereigns," said Mr Davenport.

"And nor I. But we are yet to enquire of your gardener if our vagrant did indeed complete the task as instructed. I feel that your wife may have interrupted the examination."

"Well, of course I interrupted the examination," said Mrs Davenport. "Seeing him walking back and forth like a demented idiot. I never saw anything more ridiculous in my life."

Mr Davenport turned to his wife.

"I assume that you are prepared to take responsibility for his conduct," he said.

"I take full responsibility," Mrs Davenport gave in answer. "If he walks off with the silver plate, I shall pay for its replacement out of the money that was mine before we married, and which you so graciously allow me to use."

"Then he shall stay," said Mr Davenport. "Until he walks out of his own accord."

"Which you think will be soon."

Mr Davenport drank some of his port.

"These young vagrants never stick at anything, my dear," he said, assuredly. "They have a wandering, grasshopper mind. But you are quite at liberty to discover this for yourself. Do not let me stop you."

Sam remained standing at the far end of the room, staring into space. He reflected that standing in a dining room was easier than standing over a foundry furnace. And the opinions now being voiced, although not directly to him, were no more insulting than those of the foundry workers. Yes, thought Sam, I have moved upwards.

"Could you bring me a little more cabbage," asked Mrs Davenport. Sam realized that she was speaking to him.

Sam moved at once without answering. He stood by the table between Mrs Davenport and the vegetarian visitor, holding the cabbage dish with both hands. The latter turned to him.

"I cannot believe what an improvement a brush-up has made," he commented. "Your appearance now borders on the elegant. And to think that we might take the credit for it."

"Yes, Sir," said Sam. He had seen himself in a mirror in the servants' quarters, barely recognising himself as being the same man that he had seen in rivers and windows whilst tramping towards London.

"Do you like your new life?" went on the visitor.

"Yes, Sir. I'm very grateful, Sir."

"You have no desire to return to the road?"

"No, Sir. I would not give tuppence to be back there."

"You see? What did I tell you, Davenport," said the visitor, triumphantly. "The vagrant is as easily cured of his addiction to the road as a schoolboy is cured of his inattentive mind."

"The vagrant has been here but a few hours," said Mr Davenport. "So hasty a judgement may be unwise. We are yet to discover if he will still be here tomorrow morning."

"Oh, don't be ridiculous, Davenport," said Mr Bewley. "Of course he will be here tomorrow. You just do not want to admit that your harsh opinion of those less fortunate than yourself was misguided."

"Perhaps." Mr Davenport placed his napkin upon the table in a conclusive fashion. He turned to Sam.

"What is your name, boy?"

"Samuel, Sir. Sam Brazenall."

"Would you prefer to be called Samuel or Brazenall?"

"Sam would be best, Sir."

"All right, Sam. Are you familiar with wine?"

Sam could not answer.

"Obviously not. Come with me to the wine cellar. I wish to present our visitor with some of our vintage port." He got up out of his chair; Sam followed him out of the dining room, leaving Mrs Davenport alone to entertain Mr Bewley.

"Well, I think you acted with good judgement," said Mr Bewley. "I am sure the young man will not let you down."

"I hope not. He is quite charming, do you not think?"

"I would not go as far as charming," said Mr Bewley. "Merely independent of mind. But he must be a decade younger than you."

"At least," said Mrs Davenport. "Maybe even two decades."

"Your husband seems to have taken to him. Doubtless he is now instructing him in the art of wine decantation. I do not believe I have ever before seen such rapid progress in domestic service. I suspect that it will not be long before he is promoted to the position of butler."

"Butler, footman, it is all the same in a house this

size," said Mrs Davenport. "But it is nice to have a young man around. Mrs Renshaw and Mary are acceptable as servants, but their company can be a bit wearisome at times."

"Your husband is not here in the evenings?"

"He goes to his club most days, from about four o'clock onwards. I have little with which to occupy myself. I could find something to do during the afternoon, I am sure, but in the evening there is very little that a gentlewoman can do alone."

"What would you like to do, that you cannot do alone?"

"Well, I would like to go out to the theatre or the opera from time to time. As we did when I first met Harry. But now he never asks to take me to any such places. And it does not feel right that I should ask him."

"It seems that he is taking you for granted," said Mr Bewley.

"Well, that is better than not being taken at all," said Mrs Davenport. "I am glad to be a married woman."

"To be a married woman affords much in the way of domestic comfort," said Bewley, in a positive and upbeat tone. "You have your own furnished house in what can be described as an up and coming neighbourhood."

"Alas, my husband does not actually own the house. He does not believe houses to be an investment, preferring to speculate in stocks and shares. He rents this villa at an extortionate price and must have paid at least half its value already. As for an up and coming neighbourhood, I do not believe that the right sort of people are moving into the area. The high walls and gates surrounding the houses are there for a reason."

"I'm sure there is nothing of an immoral nature going on behind them, Mrs Davenport."

"Oh, I don't mean anything quite like that. But a certain type of unmarried woman who is kept by one particular gentleman might choose St John's Wood as a place of residence, for the grounds of the villas are well-concealed so as to protect the identity of a male visitor."

"Is that so, Mrs Davenport."

"It is quite so. What is more, in the house two doors from ours, there is an unmarried couple living together as though they were man and wife. Such people are giving the area a bad name. I do not believe my husband is even aware of the existence of the problem."

"St John's Wood may have a slightly bohemian reputation," conceded Mr Bewley. "But surely the building itself is quite satisfactory; it is of ample proportions and complemented by a large garden at the back."

Mrs Davenport did not appear at all reassured. "The house is poorly constructed," she countered. "We have lived here but five years and already the doors and skirtings have shrunk. The house was new when we first moved in; everything seemed all right then, but expenses had been spared. It is the same with all the houses around here. I feel quite degraded."

"You are allowing yourself to become too depressed, Mrs Davenport."

"Oh, I am not really depressed. Just a little dissatisfied, maybe."

Mary suddenly entered the room. Mrs Davenport looked at her questioningly.

"Mrs Renshaw was wondering if you would like the desert to be sent up now," she said.

"Yes, Mary," said Mrs Davenport. Mary was about to leave. "Oh, could you tell me, how is Samuel settling in downstairs?"

"Oh, very well, Madam. Both Mrs Renshaw and I have taken a liking to him. I mean, we both get on well with him."

"Thank you, Mary," said Mrs Davenport. Mary walked towards the door again. It opened, and Sam walked in again, startling Mary. He carried a silver tray upon which stood a decanter of port and two glasses. As he placed each of the two glasses carefully at Mr Bewley and Mr Davenport's place, the master of the house walked in again.

"I thought we still had a bottle of the '39," he said, as he sat down at the table again. "But it would appear that it is drunk. I think in future, I will have to keep records of the wine in the cellar, as they do in all the good houses. Samuel, are you able to read and write?"

"Yes, Sir," said Sam. "I can read and write without any trouble."

"Well, then, can I assume you will have no trouble writing down in a cellar-book all wines ordered and drunk, and to sign your name at each entry?"

"You can, Sir."

"Then I shall have to seriously consider entrusting the task to you." Mr Davenport turned towards his guest again. "Bewley, I do apologise for being unable to offer you that exceptional vintage of '39. However, this port is nonetheless good," he said, pouring out two glasses from the decanter.

"Thank you, Davenport. You seem to be living well these days. Have your investments done well?"

"They have done acceptably well. The dramatic increases for which I was hoping have not occurred, but nevertheless I believe them to have a sound value. The stock market is yet to let me down."

"I wish I had your courage and enterprise, Davenport. I almost invested in the railways, but my wife advised against it. I could have been set up for several lifetimes."

"Well, I am not one to sit on the fence. One is apt to fall off it eventually. Although I would not actually recommend speculation to others. I would not wish to be responsible for their misfortune."

"You are quite right, Davenport. I do not recommend recommending either. But if you are prepared to take the risks of your own volition, that is quite your own affair. I wish you all the best with it."

Mr Davenport raised his glass to his guest. "That is most gratifying," he responded. "I am glad to have a friend such as you."

Bewley responded with his own raised glass.

"Always at your service, Davenport."

Sam continued to stand. Mrs Davenport appeared to be observing him again. He glanced briefly at her, then stepped back a few more paces to the sideboard.

"That will be all, Sam," said Mr Davenport. "You may go."

Sam left the room, closing the door quietly behind him.

"So, our vagrant is now a butler," said Mr Bewley. "Thanks to your fair and generous action."

"I still maintain that he will not remain so for long," said Mr Davenport. "Once a vagrant, always a vagrant."

"Well, we shall see," said Mr Bewley.

CHAPTER 7

It was usual for Cook to rise just before seven a.m. on a mid-winter morning, for, as her mistress had told her, an hour lost in the morning would keep her toiling, absolutely toiling, all day. That Monday morning she was downstairs by half-past seven; the kitchen had been swept and cleaned and the fire had been lit. She began to engage herself with numerous little preliminary occupations. The house breakfast was at eight; the servants' breakfast at half-past eight. At half-past nine she was sitting at the kitchen table, with her usual mid-morning cup of tea. But despite this temporary relaxation, she was still keeping an eye on the new footman intent on his work in the parlour. A copy of 'The Times' was to be sent up to the master. She watched as he lifted the heavy iron from the fireplace and took it over to the ironing board, on which the newspaper lay.

"This is quite a joke," said Sam, as he ran the iron over the front page. "Are you sure he wants it ironed? You'll be telling me to iron his shoe-laces next."

"Mrs Davenport instructed me when I first come here that any newspaper presented in a good house should be ironed and folded on a tray," said Cook. "Some notion she read about in a magazine, I'll be bound. As for shoe-laces, the master's very fussy about those; he doesn't bother having them laundered. He just buys new ones."

"What does he do with the old ones?"

"Mrs Davenport gives them to the poor and needy," said Cook. "A woman from Barnado's comes here once a month to collect any old clothes and unwanted items. Though now that you're here, some of it may be coming your way."

Mary appeared. "The master wants to know where the newspaper is," she said, at once. "He's waiting for it in his study."

"Sam has been out and bought it," said Cook. "He's just ironing it."

"The master wants it brought up immediately," insisted Mary. "He'd like some strong, black coffee as well."

"Well, you better start making it, my girl," said Cook, without moving. After a moment, Mary headed into the kitchen.

"I thought he worked in the City," said Sam.

"He takes a day off from time to time. To put his financial affairs in order."

"I suppose there'll be no question of me taking a day off," said Sam.

"Not at all," said Cook. "You're in quite a different situation. You need to work. The master need not work at all if he pleases. He only works half the year as it is."

"Why on earth does he bother?"

"It gives him something to pass the time."

"It's quite beyond me," said Sam. The newspaper was now in a most exquisite state. He took it into the kitchen and placed it on the silver tray, along with the coffee canister, creamer, sugar bowl with silver tongs, china cup and saucer. Mary was busy grinding the coffee. Sam went to a cupboard and took out a cloth. He picked up the coffee pot and gave it a quick polish, as he did with the rest of the silver. As soon as all was prepared he immediately carried the tray upstairs; on reaching the study he walked straight in without knocking, as instructed.

The master was sitting at his desk at the window, with his back to the door. He turned as Sam entered.

"Ah, Sam," he said in acknowledgement, taking the presented newspaper. Sam placed the coffee tray upon the desk. He was about to depart, but then the master spoke.

"Just a minute, Sam." The master was leafing through the pages of 'The Times', apparently trying to find something. Eventually, he stopped at a page with columns of numbers, set in tables. Sam waited as the master examined them. Then the master took a piece of letter paper from the leather case upon the desk and began to write.

"I want you to take this letter directly to an address in the City," he said, as he wrote rapidly. "Do you think you can manage that?"

"Of course, Sir," said Sam. He stood expectantly at the desk until the master had finished writing.

"The sooner this gets there, the better," went on the master. "Time is of the essence." And he folded up the letter, stamped it with an old-fashioned wax seal, and scribbled an address on the back. Then he handed it to Sam.

"I'll go immediately," said Sam.

"Here's a crown," said the master, producing a silver coin. "It may be quicker to take a Hansom."

Sam walked out of the room immediately, glancing at the address on the letter. It read:

For the immediate attention of
Mr George Loveless, Esquire
Stock Exchange
2 Capel Court
LONDON

He left the house by the front entrance door, an un-common practice for him. With such an urgent task to perform, it seemed forgivable. He strode briskly down Wellington Road and continued on, alongside Regent's Park. He was not quite sure of the shortest route to the City; perhaps it would be best to go to Euston Station and pick up a cab there. He hurried on, quickening his pace. A footman should not actually be seen to be running, he considered. No one stopped him to ask him what he was doing. Presumably it was quite normal for a footman to be walking through town on an errand. At one point he saw a cab heading towards him in the opposite direction; he attempted to hail it, shouting out, hi! But the cab-man did not stop; it was probably already occupied. It was of no matter; up ahead he could see three Hansom cabs, waiting in a line at the roadside by the park. The horses' heads were stuck in their nosebags, and as Sam came closer, the drivers were nowhere to be seen. Instead, an unkempt costermonger type dressed raggedly and inadequately for the winter morning was hanging around near them, leaning against the park railings.

"I need a cab, quick," said Sam, coming straight up to him.

"I daresay you do," said the unsavoury buck. "But you'll have to wait a while. They're all in the coffee shop across the road."

Sam glanced across the empty stone-laid street. A very large window displaying crockery and eatables fronted the premises of a working-class coffee house. Sam hurried across to it, narrowly avoiding a large swathe of horse dung in the middle of the road. He opened the door of the premises and entered; it was very quiet inside, and a bit shadowy and dim. The demure-looking damsel serving the coffee regarded him with perturbation. Sam looked all around him for anyone resembling a cab driver.

"I need a cab, at once," he stated in a loud voice. One drab and dreary man, dressed in what was clearly a cabman's cape, looked up from his newspaper.

"I'll pay extra if we can go now," said Sam. This was enough to get the man in motion. Standing slowly up, he took a coin from his pocket and placed it carefully onto the table. Then he followed Sam straight out of the coffee shop, into the road outside.

"Come from your master, have you?" asked the cabman, as he climbed wearily up to his seat at the back of the Hansom.

"Yes," said Sam. "Please take me directly to the Stock Exchange." He stepped up and opened the wooden half-doors, sat down on the comfortable cushioned seat within and closed the doors. The cab immediately took off with amazing speed. It was a giddy ride through the bustling city. The main streets were jammed with omnibuses, carts, carriages and wagons; but the Hansom seemed undeterred by these obstructions, weaving its way between the vehicles in a most agile manner. It could not have been more than twenty minutes before the cab finally rolled past the Bank of England and up to the door at the far end. They were in an alleyway. Opposite lay what had to be the entrance to Capel Court. Sam opened the trapdoor in the roof of the Hansom and handed the driver a crown.

"I hope that's enough," he called out.

"Oh, it's definitely enough," said the cabman. Sam jumped out into the alleyway. The cab immediately moved off before Sam asked for any change. Sam hurried into the courtyard and up to the imposing doors fronting the plain building of stone that was the London Stock Exchange. It had a central part, which appeared to have been extended both to the East and West. He walked confidently into an enormous, crowded hall with great Ionic columns on either side and a huge circular clock face upon the wall at the other end. But no sooner had he entered when he was asked by a clerk to produce his ticket.

"I have no ticket," said Sam. "I have a letter for a stockbroker here." And he held out the urgent communication sealed with Mr Davenport's impressive-looking seal.

"Oh, I see," said the official, "I'll see that it gets to him."

"I would rather deliver it myself," said Sam, withdrawing the letter.

"I'm afraid that's not possible. Only members and their clerks are allowed in here – and clerks only with their ticket. But if the stockbroker in question is here I shall see to it that he receives the letter at the first possible opportunity."

"Oh, all right," said Sam, handing it over. He gazed around, in awe of the surroundings, admiring the gallery up above equipped with desks, seats and bookcases; a clerk leant over the rail and threw a book down to a stockbroker below.

"You have to leave now," whined the official.

"I'm going," said Sam, immediately walking out into the daylight again. He went back down the alleyway and into a long street with grand palatial buildings on either side. He strolled past one stockbroker's after another, realizing that this was obviously an epicentre of finance. A feeling of security, unknown to him before, enveloped him, just from being in the place. No longer did wealth seem like such an alien concept; there was nothing extraordinary about the men who passed him; he could so easily be one of them. In a tortuous route back to St John's Wood he continued on into Bishopsgate, then down Lime Street; then into Fenchurch Street and finally ended up in a little lane which had the aroma of tea all along it. Here were many stockbrokers and tea merchants. He passed the London Commercial Salerooms and the Cloth Workers' Hall, then more stockbrokers. I shall return here in two days on my afternoon off, he decided, quickening his step again.

When he got back to the villa, he entered through the back entrance this time. He was feeling like a servant again, now. Coming straight into the kitchen he was confronted by the sight of Cook, seated at the kitchen table, as though she had never moved; but of course she must have done. She would have been up to see Mrs Davenport to receive her instructions for the day's dining arrangements. It seemed like time for a breather. He sat down opposite her and she almost automatically reached for a cup and saucer for him.

"Where have you been, Sam?" she asked, as she poured. "I haven't seen you all morning."

"Running an errand for Mr Davenport. I've been down to the City and the Stock Exchange."

"Oh, yes. I know the master likes to do a lot of stock market investing."

"Can anyone invest in the stockmarket?" asked Sam. "Like a footman, for example?"

"Oh, yes," said Cook. "I knew a footman a few years back. He made a fortune on the railways. He's living in luxury now. Bought a public-house in the West End of London. Never paid a penny in investment. He answered an advertisement in the newspaper using the headed letter paper that the mistress kept in the study, and signed it using a quill pen. They immediately allocated him the shares. Soon afterwards, they sky-rocketed. It was the time of the railway boom, you see. Thirty thousand pounds all told, was what he made."

"All just from answering an advertisement?"

"That's right," confirmed Cook, drinking tea. Sam continued to look at her, in amazement.

"I can hardly believe it," he said finally.

"It's as true as I'm sitting here. Then there were Miss Purlow, lady's maid to Mrs Fortescue. She answered an advertisement for buying shares, I can't remember what they was, addressing the letter from the house. She made a quick fortune enabling her to leave service. She's certainly not doing Mrs Fortescue's hair now."

"I never see any such advertisements."

"Well, it were all a few years back."

"And they never paid a penny for the shares?"

"Oh, no. They never had no money to pay with."

"It sounds too good to be true," said Sam. "Have you seen these people since they became rich?"

"Oh, no. They disappeared like greased lightning after making their money."

"I suppose they would do," said Sam. "I wouldn't be hanging around."

"Well, I suppose I had better be getting back to work," said Cook, standing up in a slow, reluctant fashion. "Mrs Davenport wants a cold lunch in the blue room. At least I won't have to get the stove going. That lazy housemaid takes all day over it."

"What about our lunch?"

"Oh, I'll attend to that, presently."

Sam sighed and went into his new workroom, the pantry. There up on a long wooden shelf stood six oil lamps, all waiting to be cleaned, trimmed and filled. Greengage was right. Being a footman was not all show and elegance. When in the pantry, he might just as well be a housemaid.

CHAPTER 8

That Wednesday afternoon, the only afternoon of the week that Sam could call his own, he was walking through Regent's Park, a place where citizens of all stations in life could be found: gentlemen and ladies, nurses with perambulators, office clerks, street urchins, tramps. Sam walked quickly; he was on a mission. The park was a shortcut to the City, and he did not have the money for a Hansom this time. He had four hours to get to Threadneedle Street and back. I hope that stockbrokers will talk to anybody, he thought anxiously. I am not Mr Davenport. I merely work for him. Perhaps there are prerequisites to doing business with a stockbroker. Mrs Renshaw told me that those servants were applying for shares using their master's good address. Well, I have a good address, but it is obvious from my attire that I do not either rent or own the house in which I live. I cannot believe that no money is necessary to invest. Surely they will want a deposit? And so these thoughts continued to run through Sam's head until he reached the gate of the park and was out in the streets again. Once in the square mile which constituted the City of London, he felt at home once more. Walking around the City streets, the task of choosing a stockbroker seemed beyond him. There were just too many of them. Then quickly and randomly he chose John Power, of sixty-seven Threadneedle Street. Judging from the building and the sign outside he seemed perfectly reputable. The front door was closed so he knocked loudly with the brass door knocker in the shape of a lion. A moment later a sad, downtrodden-looking man appeared before him.

"Can I help you, sir?" said the hapless clerk, standing somewhat defensively.

"I need a stockbroker," said Sam, decisively. "I want to buy some shares."

"Oh, yes sir. Well, if you would just come in and wait here for a minute, I'll see if Mr Power can speak with you. I assume you don't have an appointment."

"No," said Sam.

"Well, he might be able to spare you a few minutes. He's not too busy today."

Sam followed him into a little office that appeared also to serve as a waiting room, for there were several armless, leather upholstered chairs arranged by the wall. The clerk disappeared through a door leading into the stockbroker's office. Sam sat down. It was promising that he had not been immediately ushered out of the premises; anyone was at liberty to buy shares, so it would appear. His gaze wandered over the books and papers scattered around the dim, drab room. A clerk's life would not be for him. Far better to be a client than a clerk. And if this Power man could help him to make something out of nothing he would really start to get on top of things.

The clerk reappeared. "You're in luck, Mr Brazenall," he said. "Mr Power will see you now." The pathetic man shuffled back to his seat at the desk and sat dutifully down again.

"It's through there," he said, indicating the doorway

98

through which he had just come. Sam got up and went over to it. He stepped into a larger, darker office, where stood an enormous desk, behind which Mr Power was seated. "Do sit down, Mr Brazenall," said the dry and dusty man. "I believe you wish to purchase some shares." There was, however, nowhere to sit as the chairs were covered with books and papers.

"Oh, I am sorry," said Mr Power, getting up and removing a pile of documents from the chair on the other side of the desk. Sam sat down. "Yes," he said immediately. "I thought possibly in the railways. I believe you don't need a deposit for that."

"Oh," said Mr Power, uncertainly. He sat down again in a business-like manner opposite Sam behind his gargantuan desk. "Well, I'm afraid you may be a bit late for that. There was a boom in the railways a few years back, but it's over now. As for not paying a deposit, that may well have been true at the time. But any shares that you purchase through me will require part payment at the very least. I presume you have a bit of money put by."

"Oh, yes," Sam reassured him. "How great a part payment would be required?"

"Oh, twenty percent should be enough," said Mr Power." "But I really would not recommend shares in the railways."

"Well, what would you recommend?" asked Sam.

Mr Power sat back in his seat and raised his eyes to the ceiling in contemplation.

"It depends on what sort of investment you are looking for. There are long-term low risk investments and there are short-term, high-risk investments. I would usually recommend the former."

"Well, I think I would prefer the latter," said Sam. "Do you have any suggestions?"

"Well, if it is an investment of a speculative nature that you desire, you could do worse than Cornish copper."

"Copper? Like in a copper mine?"

"Precisely. If I had the courage to invest in copper I might well put a sum of money into Wheal Tryphena. The shares fell abruptly last week but I believe that they will very soon recover."

"Then go ahead with it," said Sam. "I'll take it."

"Certainly," said Mr Power, picking up a quill and dabbing it in the inkwell on the silver inkstand that stood upon the desk. "To what value would you like to purchase the shares?"

"Er ... twenty-five pounds," said Sam, mentally calculating twenty percent. Surely he could get his hands on five pounds somehow or other.

"Very good," said Mr Power, energetically writing down the particulars on some paper. "I shall require a deposit of five pounds, plus a commission of five shillings."

"That will be fine," said Sam. "But I cannot bring the money until next week."

"Then I shall delay the purchase until next week when my clerk will prepare the documentation for you to sign." Mr Power finished writing. He now appeared to have more pressing matters to attend to, for he put the piece of paper aside, clasped his hands together and looked expectantly at Sam.

"Until next week, Mr Brazenall," the stockbroker said, finally.

"Yes. Well, thank you very much, Mr Power," said

Sam, with a quick departure from the room. Well, that was easy, he thought to himself, as the clerk made him an appointment for the following Wednesday. This done, he walked out into the busy, narrow street again. Now that business was over, he could try out some of the local public-houses. But fearing that he might accidentally bump into Mr Power, he walked away from the City towards Regent's Park. He was due back at the house in two hours.

Where on earth was he going to get five pounds from, he wondered, as he sat in the '---' in --- street. His current remuneration amounted to twenty pounds a year – but he wanted the money by next week. Perhaps someone would lend it to him. As soon as the shares went up in value, he would repay the loan, with interest. Would a money lender help him? The prospect of approaching a cent-per-cent was not appealing. The conundrum of how to raise the initial investment continued to plague him all the way home. But somehow he knew that by next Wednesday afternoon he would have five pounds.

"Where've you been?" asked Mary, as he stepped into the servants' hall.

"You'll know soon enough," said Sam. Mary is always asking me silly questions about what I'm doing, he thought in irritation. Why is she so interested anyway? She was always fussing around him.

"I'll just take your coat," said Mary, helping him off with it.

"Thank you, Mary, but it's really not necessary," said Sam. "You're paid to look after the master and mistress, not me."

"Oh, I'll look after you for nothing," said Mary, enthusiastically.

"I was afraid of that," said Sam, walking into the parlour. Cook was putting her feet up again and as usual, drinking tea.

"The mistress was asking for you, while you were out," said Cook. "She didn't seem to be aware that it was your afternoon off."

"Well, that's strange, for it was she who allocated me my afternoon off," said Sam.

"Well, anyway, she wants to see you," said Cook.

"Me?" said Sam. "What on earth for? It's usually the master who informs me of my duties."

"I've no idea. Some whim or other, I expect."

A bell jangled from the rack above. "That'll be her now," said Cook. "You had better get going."

Sam looked up at the bell-rack. "But it's coming from her bedroom," he said, incredulously.

"Oh, is it? Well, Mary had better go up, then. Off you go, my girl."

Sam noticed that Mary was now standing in the parlour. He watched as she scampered away and up the stairs. When she was gone he sat down at the dining table.

"I wish Mary would stop following me around," he complained. "She always seems to be hovering. Whenever I'm in the parlour, she's in the parlour. Always trying to engage me in meaningless conversation. I'm becoming entirely sick of it."

"Well, it's only to be expected," said Cook. "A young man like yourself, working in the household. She doesn't get that many opportunities."

"I am not an opportunity," said Sam.

"Well, she doesn't know that. She's hoping to snap you up."

"Really?" said Sam. "I didn't realize she was that interested in me."

"Oh, she's definitely interested. She's hoping for nothing less than marriage, I'll be bound."

"Mary wants to marry me? How amazing."

"Oh, there's nothing amazing about it. There's nothing more attractive to a girl in service than the prospect of marriage." Upon this thought, Cook got out of her chair. "I've got the dinner to see to now," she said. "Mrs Davenport will be dining alone, as usual. It's about as much work to prepare a dinner for one as it is for ten."

Sam remembered the row of boots in the back parlour that he had been halfway through polishing before he had left the house. He wandered over to the pantry. But just at this moment, Mary's shrill voice broke into the air.

"Sam! The mistress wants to see you in her boudoir," she called out from halfway down the stairs.

"Oh, very well," said Sam. He turned around and went upstairs.

Mrs Davenport was sitting before her mirror at her dressing table, brushing her hair slowly and methodically. She saw Sam in the mirror as he entered and turned to see him.

"Sam. I called for you earlier, but you weren't here."

"It was my afternoon off, Madam," explained Sam, apologetically.

"Yes, of course." She continued to brush her hair. There was a silence. Finally, she put down the brush.

"Are you settling in well, Sam?"

"Yes, Madam. Everything is to my satisfaction."

"Do you get on well with the other servants?"

"Yes, Madam. They're all very friendly."

"Good. I sent for you earlier this afternoon because I had some business to attend to in town that requires the services of my footman. However, you had already gone out. I have now had to postpone it until next Wednesday afternoon. I trust that you will be available then?"

"If you so wish it, Madam," said Sam.

"I shall of course provide you with extra remuneration."

"Thank you, Madam."

Mrs Davenport picked up the brush again. "Very well then, Sam. I want you to meet me at Mivart's hotel at one o'clock next Wednesday. Are you familiar with Mivart's?"

"No. I've never heard of it, Madam."

"It is situated in Brook Street, Mayfair, in the vicinity of Grosvenor Square. You can not fail to see it – a hotel of that size."

"I'm sure I'll find it, Madam."

"There is also one other thing. The business that I wish to attend to in the hotel is of a private nature. I shall therefore be using another name. When you arrive at the hotel, you must announce that you are there to see Mrs Darnley, and that you are her footman.

"Mrs Darnley, Madam?"

"That is correct. Do you think that you can remember that?"

"Without any trouble, Madam."

"Good. Well then, that will be all, Sam."

Sam left the room directly. Mrs Davenport had

mentioned extra remuneration. How much extra? It would not have done to ask. He returned to the parlour in the servants' hall, where Mary was laying out the plates and cutlery for supper. She seemed to be ignoring him, now. Was it really true that Mary was so enamoured with him? He was not sure. He walked into the kitchen, on his way to the boots in the back room. Cook was occupied at the work table.

"What did Mrs Davenport want?" she asked abruptly.

"Oh, she just wanted to know how I was getting on," said Sam. "She likes to think that her servants are all reasonably happy."

"Very considerate of her, I'm sure," said Cook.

Sam went into the back room and started on the boots again. He picked up an elegant lady's boot obviously belonging to Mrs Davenport and placed it carefully onto the unusual contraption provided to keep the lining free of dirty hand marks, so offensive to a lady of refined tastes. Then, with the utmost delicacy, he began to polish the leather, until the upper part had the freshest of an appearance. But even this light work was now irksome to him. I have become a Weary Willie, he thought, glumly. Any work is now too great a task for me. I just hope that the extra remuneration that I am to receive will amount to something. I cannot go on like this. A man in service is no better than a slave. And so he continued to think as the week went by, only vaguely aware of the impending appointment with Mrs Davenport.

That Wednesday afternoon at one o'clock, he set off towards Mayfair. He hurried quickly through the busy thoroughfares, not quite sure of his way and asking for directions as he went. Eventually he reached Grosvenor Square, then Brook Street. On the corner stood a tall, wide Georgian residence that most obviously constituted Mivart's Hotel. Sam crossed the road just as a carriage pulled up outside the portico. He felt that he should rush to open the carriage door, but then remembered that his current duty was to enter the hotel under the identity of Mrs Darnley's footman. Entering the elegant building he was greeted civilly by the doorman, whereupon another member of staff appeared. Sam told this gentleman that he was there on Mrs Darnley's request.

"Are you her footman? Yes, she told us that she was expecting you," said the manager politely. "Have you brought her luggage?"

"The luggage is being sent on," said Sam. He did not know what else to say.

"Jones will show you to the room," said the hospitable man. Jones appeared. He was neither young nor old and of a non-descript appearance. Dressed in a superior uniform based on eighteenth century mode he guided Sam up the elegant stairway. It seemed strange for one footman to be following another. When they reached the door, Jones hovered, expectantly.

"I'm sorry, I don't have any money," said Sam, his accent returning. The hotel footman departed ungraciously. Sam knocked softly on the door.

"Come in," came Mrs Davenport's familiar voice.

Sam gently pushed open the mahogany door. Mrs Davenport was lying in the sumptuous bed provided, half-undressed amongst pillows, sheets and covers. Upon the bedside table lay a large, white five pound note. Sam closed the door behind him and locked it.

At twenty-five to four, Sam was off through the park again, towards the City. At last, spring had arrived and it produced within him a spring in his step. People seemed to notice his joyous state – everyone appeared to be looking at him as he marched briskly down Throgmorton Street, past the Bank of England again and into Threadneedle Street. At his stockbroker's – he had already become used to referring to Mr Power as 'his stockbroker' – he surprised the same clerk with his second coming.

"Mr Power about?" he asked, in a voice full of cheer and confidence.

"Oh, yes. He's in his office now. Do you wish to see him? Your appointment was at three." The clerk, whose name was still unknown to Sam, stood up in expectation.

"Yes, I know, but I was unavoidably detained," said Sam. "Is it still possible for me to see him? It's rather urgent."

"I'll go and ask him," said the clerk, obligingly. He disappeared through the door opposite. Through the window, the sun came glaring through. The clerk emerged a moment later. "Yes, he'll see you now," he said, propping the door open. Sam walked in. Mr Power was looking up from writing something. Sam sat down eagerly opposite his stockbroker. Without hesitation, he placed the sheet of paper which was nothing less than a five pound note of the Bank of England in front of him. But Mr Power did not appear quite so enthusiastic.

"I'm sorry I'm late," said Sam. "I really could not help it. I am in service, you see."

"Yes, I know," said Mr Power. "Mr Brazenall, I was pressed for time the last time I saw you and failed to explain the full situation." Sam froze in alarm.

"I really should have made things a bit clearer," the man went on. "I failed to mention that although only a deposit for the shares is initially required, a demand for the entire capital can be made at any time."

"Oh," said Sam. "What would happen if the demand was not met?"

"Well, if the shares had lost in value, it could mean a debtor's prison."

"Oh," said Sam again.

"However, if you still wish to proceed, I would be happy to arrange the transaction."

"Yes," said Sam. "I do wish to proceed."

"Very well, then. Does this money include or exclude the commission?"

"Includes, I suppose," said Sam.

Mr Power took the note and began writing out the documentation. At one point he stopped writing and looked up at Sam.

"Are you able to sign your own name?"

"Oh, yes," said Sam.

Fifteen minutes later, Sam was walking out of the stockbroker's office. Out in the daylight again he held before him the documented certification of the trans-action: it was headed, 'a scrip certificate for forty shares in Wheal Tryphena'. It was more than just a piece of paper; it was a symbol of unbridled wealth. When the share value rose, he would cash it in, thereby producing something out of nothing. In the meantime, he would try and raise the capital required for the full amount – just in case the share value should fall and the demands were made. Visions of Bridewell appeared before his eyes; would they have a treadwheel in a debtor's prison? He did not know and did not want to know. At least incarceration in Bridewell was a temporary affair; but once in debt, how would he ever come out of it? He would remain in the debtor's prison forever.

As he wandered back to his place of employment, he considered each and every possible way in which he might acquire the full value of the shares, but none seemed viable save one. Mrs Davenport was not such a bad woman; in exchange for extra remuneration, he supposed that he could put up with her for a little while.

CHAPTER 9

Some weeks later, around ten thirty at the end of a long day, Sam was finally alone in the pantry that also served as his sleeping quarters. He had closed the shutters that covered the small grated windows and lit the candle provided, producing a sad glow all around. The washed silver cutlery was laid out on the long table in the middle of the room, to be polished first thing tomorrow. As usual, he moved the closet bedstead across the doorway, whereupon he sat down upon it and began to undress.

The only problem with Mrs Davenport is that my Wednesday afternoons are now gone, he considered, taking off his boots and placing them neatly at the foot of the bed. But if I am to avoid any possibility of the debtor's prison, so it must be. Impulsively, he got up in his stockings and went over to where his long greatcoat hung; he felt the lining into which he had sewn four large bank notes and was reassured that they appeared to be still there. He was content merely to visualise the handsome appearance of these clean, white sheets of parchment, upon which was ornately written in copper plate writing, 'I Promise to pay Mrs Davenport or Bearer on Demand the Sum of Five Pounds'. He then went back and continued to undress and don his nightshirt, after which he fell upon his bed, slipping almost immediately into a deep and restful sleep, only to be awakened in a manner most harsh eight hours later, by Mary's loud, irritating knock upon the door.

"Half-past six," her shrill voice rang out. She did that every morning. She never entered, however. Sam opened his eyes and thought he could see smoke; but when he opened the shutters he realised that it was fog. Closing the shutters again he went to put on his stockings and boots; not ten minutes later he was dressed, and set to work polishing the silver. It was definitely above freezing this morning but still very cold. Soon after, Mary came in, placing her housemaid's box on a piece of coarse cloth beside the grate.

"How comes you never gets any of the nasty jobs?" she enquired, as she began sweeping up the ashes, with her back to him.

"I can't answer questions this early," said Sam. His thoughts returned to high finance. Perhaps I should have consulted Mr Davenport on the subject of speculation, he thought suddenly. But no, it was better to go about things entirely independently. And it was good to know that anyone could invest, not just the likes of Mr Davenport. He became aware that Mary had left the room and now he was starting to feel very drowsy again. I really feel like having another sleep, he almost said out loud. He heard Cook, working in the kitchen next door, and Mary setting out the breakfast things. They always had tea for breakfast, which was a terrible shame, for tea really was not his drink. It sedated rather than invigorated. If I had stayed in the foundry, I would now be having a large canister of coffee, he thought, regretfully. That had been a highlight of foundry life, along with The

Red Lion. Here I cannot drink at any time, not even in the evening. Perhaps that is a good thing, perhaps not. I cannot say I feel the better for having given up drink.

"Breakfast's ready, Sam," called out Mary, from the kitchen. When he did not come immediately, she popped her head around the door. Sam glanced uninterestedly at her.

"Coming," he said.

She came into the pantry again. "You've certainly got your work cut out today," she observed, picking up a silver ladle.

"You've noticed that, have you," said Sam.

"I've noticed a lot of things about you," said Mary, glancing at him in a manner that Sam believed was described as 'coy'.

"Have you," said Sam. He picked the piece of soft rag that appeared to be the top of an old stocking and dabbed it into the paste.

"And I reckons there's more to you than meets the eye."

"I don't meet the eye much, do I?"

"Well, you're the quiet type. But I think there's a strong man in there, waiting to get out."

"Is that so."

"Perhaps we could walk out one day, on your afternoon off."

"I don't think so."

"Where do you go on your afternoons off?"

"Wouldn't you like to know."

"I doubt if you go anywhere special. You're probably really bored, on your own."

"I am indeed," said Sam, standing up. He walked past

Mary and into the dining area, glancing up through the bars across the windows to the pavement above. The residence of the Davenports was no less a prison than the iron foundry, just a little more genteel. Then he sat down at the dining table and stretched out his legs underneath it.

"Don't look so miserable, Sam," said Cook. "It's an annoyance to have a misery around."

"Cheer me up, then," said Sam, leaning back on the uncomfortable wooden chair. "If you can." But he knew there was no real reason for despondency. His current situation was but a temporary one. The following week, on his afternoon off, instead of going straight to Mivart's, he would head for the city, to see Mr Power again. Once the full amount of the shares were paid, he would have no cause to worry.

It was not long before Wednesday afternoon came round. Sam omitted to turn up at Mivart's, but instead, proceeded directly to the City. For the third time Sam sat across the desk from his stockbroker.

"As you see, I have the full amount," he was saying, proffering the five-pound notes which he was sure that Mr Power had never expected to see. "I do not relish the thought of admittance to a debtor's prison."

"So you do," said Mr Power. "But I think that in your case, the debtor's prison is unlikely. The market has been generally buoyant since we last spoke. And your shares have done particularly well. It was at thirty pence that you bought them, was it not?" He was searching for some documentation amongst the mass of papers upon his desk.

"Yes," said Sam, expectantly.

"Well, this morning they were worth eighty."

"Eighty?"

"That is correct."

"I had no idea what they were worth. I had no way of finding out, other than by coming here."

"Share listings for the mining industry are to be found in the Railway and Commercial Gazette, available from railway stations and booksellers," said Mr Power.

"Oh! I shall remember that, in future," said Sam.

"If I were you, I should sell your shares now," said Mr Power. "Copper is fickle. One day it is up, the next it is falling."

"Yes, please sell them for me," said Sam. "The sooner, the better. You can take this money if needs be."

"No, it is not required," said Mr Power. "Have you brought the scrip certificate?"

Sam immediately produced it.

"If you would be good enough to return in an hour, I should have confirmed the transaction by then," said Mr Power. "I just need your signature, and I shall go at once to the Stock Exchange."

Sam signed the parchment that was thrust before him. He could hardly imagine the money; it would be more than he had ever seen before in his life. As soon as Mr Power gave him the cash he would go straight back to St John's Wood to collect his things.

Entering the servants' hall through the area, the staff lunch was in preparation. I don't think I'll have time for that, he thought, even though hungry. He was walking through the parlour towards the pantry to hurry when Cook stopped him.

"Is anything the matter, Sam?" he heard her ask.

Sam turned to her.

"What? Oh, no, absolutely nothing. I've just decided to leave, that's all."

"Leave? Without a good-bye or by-your-leave?"

"That's absolutely correct. I'm not staying here a minute longer."

"Will the master let you leave, at such short notice?"

"He won't have any choice."

"You won't get a character," said Cook, with conviction.

"Don't need one. I'm independent – at least, for a little while."

"Independent? What on earth do you mean?"

"Exactly what I say. I've got some money put by."

"Good heavens," said Cook. "Well, I never. So you've come into a bit of money," she said, turning back to the stove.

"You could say that," said Sam, continuing to stand. "Has Mrs Davenport been informed?"

"Not yet," said Sam. "Apparently she has gone out until this evening."

"She'll be sorry to see you leave," said Cook. "I believe she took a shine to you."

"Yes, I believe she did," said Sam.

"Well, don't let us keep you," said Cook. "Are you staying for dinner?"

"No, I'm afraid not," said Sam. "I want to be away as soon as possible. I am a little concerned about how Mrs Davenport is going to react when she finds me gone."

"Have you got any lodgings?"

"No, but I'm sure I'll be all right."

"Well, you must have come into a quite decent sum of money, then," said Cook.

"Well, it won't last forever. I won't have to work for a while, though."

"What are you going to do when the money runs out?"

"I prefer not to think about that," said Sam. "It will last six months, possibly a year. I am sure I will have thought of something in that time. Something will come up."

"I wouldn't mind having an holiday for a year," said Cook. "The longest I ever had off was a week. It went by in a flash – seemed to be over no sooner had it started."

"I had eight months off before I came here," said Sam. "But I was not living in the utmost of comfort."

"Greengage told me about your vagabond past," said Cook. "And I'm not sure I entirely approve. It's them workhouses what's causing the vagabond lifestyle – giving out free food and shelter to anyone what wants it. In my day you either worked or you starved."

"I don't particularly appreciate either working or starving," said Sam. "And I have found that making money was actually a lot easier than I thought it was. I hope never to work again."

"I don't mean to be inquisitive, but if you don't mind my asking, where exactly did you get your money from?" asked Cook.

"I made a wise investment," said Sam. "Just like the footman you told me about, and your lady's maid friend."

"Well," said Cook. "If this carries on, there won't be anyone left in service."

"You could try some investing yourself, Cook," said Sam. "It really isn't difficult."

"No, it's not for me," said Cook. "I have heard that fortunes have been lost overnight with them stocks and shares. It's a double-edged sword, those investment things. I only hope the master isn't investing more that he can afford to lose. Mrs Davenport isn't at all happy about his gambling on the stock market. If he goes down, I'll have to look for another place. Though I suppose there's plenty of places for cooks in big houses."

"It's not gambling," said Sam. "You have stockbrokers to advise you."

"Stockbrokers don't care if shares are going up or down. Either way they still get their money."

"Well, I don't think I'll need to do any more investing for a while," said Sam. "I've got enough." He got up from the table. "I think I'll go and get my things together. I don't suppose you would have such a thing as an old carpet bag? I'm at a loss as to how I shall pack."

"There might be one in the store room. The mistress keeps telling me to give away anything old and shabby to Barnado's. I expect you can take it. Shall I let her know that you have gone?"

"You may tell her whatever you like," said Sam. "Thank you very much, Cook. I mean, Mrs Renshaw." Not sure exactly what else to say in departure, other than goodbye, he left the parlour, bumping into Mary in the doorway. He hurried out of her way with a hasty 'excuse me' and for the last time into the pantry. Then on the other side of the closed door, he could hear her in animated discussion with Cook, presumably regarding himself. The sooner he was away, the better. This was definitely a good time to disappear. I am not giving a month's notice, he thought, adamantly. It was not five minutes before he hurried out of the pantry, out of the basement door and along the driveway but was dismayed to see Mr Davenport coming in through the gate. The master must have decided to leave work early.

"Sam?" he called out inquiringly, shutting the gate behind him. "May I ask where you are going?"

Sam stopped, resignedly. Mr Davenport stepped over to him.

"I am leaving," said Sam, in as final a tone as he could muster.

"Leaving? Are you sure that's what you want?"

"I am certain," said Sam. "Would it be all right if I left immediately?"

"Well, I suppose we can manage without you – we always did before you came. Why the sudden hurry to be out of here? Have you found a new position?"

"I don't need one," said Sam. "I have some resources."

"Well, I hope these resources are substantial, for they will not last very long, otherwise," said Mr Davenport. "However, your affairs are none of my business. If you wish to leave at once, I will not stand in your way."

"Oh, thank you very much, Sir," said Sam. "If I thought I was really needed here, I would have stayed, but I seemed to be something of an extra."

"Quite so," said Mr Davenport. "It was really on account of my wife that we got a footman. I have always found the idea of footmen faintly ridiculous."

"You could say that," said Sam.

"Well, you better be off then, as you seem to be in rather a hurry," said Mr Davenport, obligingly. "It was a pleasure to make your acquaintance. Perhaps we shall meet again some day."

"Yes, perhaps," said Sam. Mr Davenport was now looking at him as though that was the end of the conversation, so he began to walk towards the main entrance gate of the grounds. Lifting the latch, he came out into the street and hurried rapidly down the Road, turning off at the end in the direction of King's Cross. What he wanted right now was lodgings on the New Road, close to the Adam and Eve public-house; that place which he had visited on one sole occasion, to be given a glimpse of how his life should have been. Would the woman ever return? It seemed unlikely; but with the whole of London to choose from, the New Road was the only place he wanted to be. If the vision of loveliness was ever to reappear in the inn, he would be ready for her. She had never heard him speak with the voice of a Somerset iron founder and she never would. A new suit of clothes, of a material and cut of his own choosing, would make him indistinguishable from the gentleman he had seen with her, the one who had been so privileged to be in her company. He felt for the wad of bank notes now in his jacket pocket, and a feeling of insecurity began to plague him. Perhaps it would be a good idea to deposit the whole amount into a bank at the first opportunity.

CHAPTER 10

It was Saturday.

"Did you say you'd come from Mrs Ratcliffe's agency?" enquired the landlady of a semi-respectable lodging-house, situated a stone's throw from the New Road. "I thought I was no longer on her books. It's been some time since I heard from them."

"That's right," said Sam, standing in the dim hallway. "They gave me the addresses of several lodgings, but I prefer the location of this one. I like the ambience."

"Well, that's the first time I've ever heard anyone say that," said the landlady. "Most people find it terribly dirty and noisy around here."

"Oh, I like the dirt and the noise," said Sam. "I hear they're building a new station at King's Cross."

"Yes, they are. The railway company has been told they can't come any farther into London than King's Cross. In a few years there'll be trains rumbling in all night and none of us will get any sleep."

"Oh, I like the sound of trains," said Sam. "They make me feel drowsy."

"You seem to like everything," said the landlady. "Would you like me to show you the room? It's at the top of the house, so you'll be well out of the way."

"I'll take it," said Sam. "Would I be able to move in today?"

"Well, I don't see why not. Are you sure you don't want to see it first?"

"I'm sure it will be perfectly all right," said Sam.

"Of course it will," said the landlady. "But I must inform you that these are respectable lodgings, and there is a no drinking rule on the premises."

"Oh," said Sam. "Do all respectable lodging-houses have a no drinking rule?"

"No," said the landlady. "But they soon will have."

"Well, in any case, you don't need to worry about that," said Sam. "I only drink in taverns. Shall I go up?"

"Yes. It's two floors up, at the top of the stairs, on the right. The privy is next door to it."

Sam sprung up the narrow, gloomy staircase until he reached the assigned door. He pushed it open to reveal a reasonably sized room, furnished only with the bare essentials. The stuffy atmosphere compelled him to open the window. The street below was quiet, but the not too distant sounds of the traffic along New Road wafted in with the breeze.

The room was certainly an improvement on a three-penny lodging-house. His own space, at last. But for how long? At a shilling a night, a year, at least. A whole year. That was eternity. He felt almost bored. Then he thought again of the Adam and Eve; he regarded himself pensively in the cracked mirror on the wall, wondering what impression he would make upon the woman should she ever miraculously return. If she did not, finding her would be like looking for a needle in a haystack. Picking up the towel that lay on the bed, he went to the wash closet and found it to be very well equipped with a sink, running water and miraculously, a water closet. He would soon be ready. The day before he had purchased a second-hand suit that was in almost immaculate condition and fitted him rather well. A quarter of an hour later he was standing in his room again, feeling like a new man. He went downstairs.

"Would you like payment in advance?" asked Sam cheerfully, as he passed his new landlady in the hallway.

"That would be very convenient. If you would."

"There you are." Sam handed over the coins. "Two weeks deposit and two weeks in advance. That's twenty-eight shillings in total."

"Thank you very much, Mr Brazenall. You're a real gentleman."

"I hope so," said Sam. "I truly hope so." He walked out into the street with what he hoped was an air of wealth and power. The lilt in his step continued all along the New Road until he reached the doors of the Adam and Eve. Perhaps the proprietor would know something about the woman. It was as crowded as it had been when he was there before, in a less than prepossessing state. But now, like a discerning customer he strode confidently into the back parlour and glanced over to the distinctive corner where the woman and her friend had been seated – to his utmost surprise, they were sitting there now, as though they had never left. As Sam sat down again at the same table by the door, it was as though time had stood still. I am to be given a second chance, he thought. And already his luck seemed to have changed. The woman was smiling at him. The man also turned to look inquiringly at Sam, then back to the woman.

"Do you know that man sitting by the entrance?" he now seemed to be asking her."

"No, I've never seen him before in my life," was her apparent answer.

"Well, he seems to know you," he was sure to be saying. The man turned to look at Sam again, this time, pronouncedly. Sam stood up and walked over to their table.

"I believe I have seen you in here before," said Sam, beaming amiably at the woman. There was now no trace of a Somerset accent in his speech.

"That would not be at all surprising," said she, viewing him in a not altogether displeased fashion. "For we are in here almost every day." And she continued to look at Sam.

"May I join you?" asked Sam, brazenly.

"Why ever not?"

Sam sat down at the unoccupied side of the table, between the man and the woman. He ignored the man. Turning again to the woman, he commented on the frosty March mornings of the last few days.

"Oh, quite so," said the woman. "It has been quite foggy and dewy in the mornings. But I do believe that April will be a fine month."

"Oh, to be in England, now that April's there," said Sam. He was not sure where he had heard this, but the line had stuck in his mind.

"That is a poem, is it not?"

"Yes, I believe it is," said Sam.

"I think we should go," came the man's voice. He was getting up to leave. "Come along, Victoria."

Sam looked at the woman. She did not appear to be moving.

"Get up at once, Victoria," persisted the man. Still she did not move.

"Well, if that is how you feel, you can escort yourself home," said the man. "I will see you tomorrow." He walked straight out of the premises, without looking back. The woman stared after him.

"Is he always like that?" asked Sam.

"Yes, usually," said the woman. He now had a chance to really study her.

"I presume that you are not married to him."

The woman sighed heavily. "My father will not allow me to marry a man of his moderate means," she seemed to allow herself to say.

"His moderate means?"

"Yes. With only a thousand pounds to his name, my father considers him to be a pauper." Sam gulped inwardly.

"In your father's eyes, what would be a reasonable amount of money for you to marry on?"

"Oh, nothing less than two thousand pounds, I should think. My father does not believe that two can live as cheaply as one." Her blue eyes seemed to be turning grey now, with black specks radiating out from her pupils and two black circles outlining her irises. Sam thought of his sixty-six pounds. It didn't seem like the time to mention it.

"Do you live with your father?" he asked, instead.

"Yes, I do. In Hampstead."

"And what brings you to this den of inequity every day?"

"I am a clerical assistant," she said, abruptly. There was a silence.

"You are jesting," said Sam.

"I'm afraid not. The men whom I work for said that employing a woman would be greatly economical to them, for they would only have to pay half the amount that a man in my position would be paid."

"And you still accepted the position?"

"I was not able to negotiate a higher salary. So yes, I accepted it. And what, if I may ask, are you doing here?"

"Me?" Sam had not considered this situation. "Er ... well, I just came into some money, so I decided to retire from my profession. I have found temporary lodgings a block or so from here until I find something more suitable."

"Somewhere more suitable?"

"Yes. I thought the Albany would be nice. It would be more convenient than a hotel." Somewhere, in his experience of London, he had heard of this place, knowing only that it was a residence for single gentlemen. "Although I suppose Mivart's does have its merits."

"Mivart's? My goodness. Have you actually stayed there?"

"Oh, yes," said Sam. "On several occasions."

"What is it like?"

"Like an elegant town house, only bigger."

"It sounds wonderful."

"I suppose it is. Although I have also had good reports from Brown's," went on Sam, in careless abandon. "But all I really want is a little flat somewhere. Perhaps Chelsea would suit me better."

"Chelsea is very fashionable," said the woman, now known to Sam as Victoria. "I would love to live in Chelsea."

"Perhaps you will, some day," said Sam. The only thing that stood between him and Victoria was one thousand nine hundred and thirty-four pounds.

"How long will you stay in your temporary lodgings?"

"Not too long, I hope," replied Sam.

"What was your profession?"

"I was in the iron industry," answered Sam, after a moment's hesitation.

"Oh, how interesting. Did you build bridges?"

"I am not an engineer," said Sam. "I was more involved in the commercial side of things. I am glad to be rid of it. I found the whole affair rather distasteful. But do tell me more about yourself. How do you spend your evenings? I trust they do not keep you at … who was it that you said you worked for?"

"I didn't. I work for a tea-dealing company near here. No, I do not work past six o'clock any evening. After dinner at home, I like to play the piano."

"Oh, really? Is that not a lonely way to spend the evening?"

"No. I obtain great solace from music. Sometimes, I sing as well."

Sam wondered what it would be like, to wander around Hampstead in the evening, with the sound of women's voices and pianos wafting through the windows of the detached residences. "What sort of music do you play?" he asked.

"Baroque, mainly. But also some modern works, such as those by Liszt and Chopin. They are terribly difficult, though."

"I'm afraid I have not heard of either of those composers," said Sam. "In fact, I have to admit that I have heard very little music during my life."

"How strange. Did you not have a piano at home?"

"No, I don't believe I did."

"I thought that all good houses had pianos."

"All good houses except ours. My parents were not interested in culture."

"How dreadful!"

"Yes, I suppose it was. But now I am in London, I shall rectify the situation immediately by attending concerts, theatres, the opera ..."

"The opera? Do you mean The Royal Italian Opera?"

"Oh, yes."

"I would so love to go to the opera. But the tickets are just a little too expensive for me. And Charles won't pay for the opera. It's too expensive for him, too."

"Well, it is not too expensive for me," said Sam. "When would you like to go?"

"Do you really mean it?"

"Of course," said Sam. "Or I would not say so."

"Well, in that case, I do not mind saying that I could go tonight. That is if you can get tickets. I believe that tonight is the opening night of their season." She seemed unnaturally excited.

"Well, then we shall go tonight," said Sam, most confidently. He stood up. "I shall go at once to make the arrangements. Where would you like me to collect you?"

"At the venue would be quite all right," she said.

"Then we shall meet again at seven o'clock outside the Royal Italian Opera House," he said, pushing the chair in again. "Goodbye until then, Victoria." And before anything could go wrong, he left the Adam and Eve without any more ado.

The Royal Italian Opera was located near the Haymarket he knew, and his nimble feet now took him in the direction of the West End. Would she really be there at seven o'clock, as promised? It all seemed too good to be true. After the performance, he would take her out to dine somewhere. As he came into the vicinity of the theatre, he passed by a fishmonger's which was also, as he now realized, a supper room. In the window were displayed semi-circles of crabs lying on their backs with lemons between their black-tipped claws, and mounds of prawns piled up in pink pyramids. There even appeared to be opera tickets for sale alongside the fish; Sam looked closely at the displayed piece of card – 'Les Metamorphoses, P. Taglioni, 16th March 1850, price 8s 6d.' That wasn't too bad. Then he noticed that the admission was for the pit. It would not be appropriate to install Victoria in the pit. The stalls were the very least he could do for her, even if the tickets were three times as expensive. Perhaps they had such tickets within. He stepped inside the premises and was immediately hit by the overwhelming fishy aroma. The place was empty, but everything was laid out.

"May I help you, sir?" enquired a voice, as he closed the door behind him. When he turned around, he perceived what seemed to be a waiter hovering at the back of the unlit room.

"Er, yes," said Sam. "You have some opera tickets in your window. I don't suppose you have any for the stalls, do you?"

"Opera tickets?" queried the man. He emerged from the shadows. "Oh, no, those tickets are for a ballet at Her Majesty's Theatre tonight."

"A ballet? But I thought there was an opera on there tonight."

"No, sir," said the man.

"There must be," said Sam. "It is the opening night of the Royal Italian Opera tonight."

"Is it?" said the man, straightening a napkin on the table near to him. He appeared to have lost interest in Sam. But as Sam went to leave, the man said, "The Royal Italian Opera is in Covent Garden."

"Oh, thank you," said Sam. "I'm much obliged to you." And he stepped out of the shop again, into the thoroughfare. How silly of him not to have known that the opera house was in Covent Garden. Well, there was no reason why he should have known. His specialist knowledge was confined to workhouses and asylums. But Covent Garden was just a stone's throw away, and he was there in no time at all. He walked across its paved square and under the cloth of the colonnade, past a small garden of flower pots that were still for sale even at this late hour. Between the pillars were the coffee stalls, with their large tin cans and piles of bread and butter, protected from the wind by paper screens and sheets thrown over clothes-horses. He was tempted to sit inside one of these little parlours but walked straight on to the theatre; it was as grand a place as he had expected; a generous, elegant building with four great columns at the entrance. In two hours time, Victoria would be standing right here. It was quiet on the pavement now, but in two hours it would no doubt be thronging with a better class of person.

I must get going, thought Sam. There is still quite a lot to be done. I do not believe it will all come to more than six pounds, he assured himself as he went unashamedly into the Royal Italian Opera, Covent Garden. He found himself within a grand entrance hall with a raised ceiling supported by pillars. There was a long queue on one side, presumably for tickets. Sam joined it. He still could not believe that Victoria really had agreed to allow him to escort her to the opera. Was he going to make a bad impression? He had no knowledge of music; but then, neither had he professed to have any. When he heard someone behind him comment that the production that he would be seeing was over three hours long, he felt in no way perturbed; it could be a hundred hours long, as long as he was in Victoria's company. It was just after five o'clock now. As the queue edged forwards, he began to forget where he was, becoming lost in anticipative dreams of the forthcoming evening and had to be jogged into consciousness again on reaching the box office window. Hereupon it seemed wholly inappropriate to install Victoria in anything less than the first tier boxes, which came to the immodest sum of twenty shillings. As he moved away from the conglomeration of opera goers and out into the street again he wondered if he had done the right thing; but then put the matter out of his mind in order to deal with more pressing issues, such as opera attire and supper rooms. It was starting to become almost like hard work. There were but two hours to spare. Not a great deal of time, but enough to partake of coffee at one of the coffee stalls. When he got to them, they appeared to be packing up for the day; however, one customer was still seated underneath the tarpaulin, sitting on a basket, drinking out of a mug. The coffee stall-keeper appeared like one who had roughed it a bit.

"I would like a cup of coffee and a ham sandwich," said Sam. "If that is possible."

"Oh, yes, sit yourself down." Sam sat down upon the bench provided.

"It is a while since I have drunk coffee," he said, as the man turned the tap of a barrel.

"Well, then you will like it all the more."

"Is it a good living, being a coffee-stall keeper?"

"It is a better living than I ever had before. I was on the brink of starvation before I began." He handed Sam the mug. "Threepence, if you please, Sir."

Sam handed over the paltry sum.

"Going to the opera, are you sir?" enquired the stall keeper.

"Yes," said Sam, drinking. The coffee tasted a little strange, as though it might have been adulterated in some way. "I am not particularly interested in the opera. But tonight I have the good fortune of escorting a young lady, and it is her pleasure to attend the Royal Italian Opera."

"Rich, is she?"

"Not really. I am paying. Though I must confess, it is heavy on my pocket. I may have to open a coffee-stall myself."

The beginnings of a smile crept over the stall-keeper's grim countenance. "Women are always heavy on the pocket. If it wasn't for women, I don't think I would have ended up here."

The coffee was starting to have its usual, enthusing effect. "She is quite wonderful," elaborated Sam. "Not at all like the women that I have met before."

"I'm sure she is. And a damned sight more expensive."

"Well, I shall just have to ensure that my resources meet her requirements," said Sam. "Do you happen to know if there is a shop around here which rents out opera attire?"

"I don't know about that," said the stall-keeper. "But there may be a pawnbroker in the Strand. There is no guarantee that the clothes will fit you, though."

"Well, I suppose I could always go as I am in the suit I have on," said Sam. "It does not really matter what I wear, I don't think."

"Really?"

"Yes. She seemed to genuinely like me."

"That's as maybe," said the stall-keeper. "But you need to dress up proper nonetheless."

"Why?"

"Clothes represent wealth," stated the stall-keeper, slowly and emphatically. "If you wear the right clothes, she will see her future as bright and prosperous; wear the wrong ones, and she will know that a life of poverty awaits her."

"Perhaps you're right," said Sam. "I think I had better hurry. All the shops will be closing soon. It's Saturday."

"Yes, I think you'd better," said the stall-keeper. Sam drank the rest of the coffee and placed the mug down upon the bench. He hurried into the Strand, where a multitude of shops was offering practically any kind of service imaginable; printsellers, trunk manufacturers, bootmakers, watchmakers and the Labouring Classes Improvement Society, whatever that was. As he continued on along the crowded pavement, he passed the offices of the Morning Chronicle, that establishment which had resulted in his rapid elevation of status. Up ahead was a pawnbroker, next door to a clothier. If the clothes did not fit, there was still just enough time to find a tailor to alter them. He imagined Victoria waiting for him in all her glory outside the Royal Italian Opera and went about the business with a renewed vigour so great, that at ten minutes to seven, he was standing by the railings of the appointed venue, dressed immaculately and smiling. Victoria had not yet arrived. He was expecting her to emerge from a carriage as it rolled up at the entrance, but she took him by surprise, suddenly appearing on foot and coming from the opposite direction to which he was looking. As she approached, he felt that she could not fail to find him acceptably presentable and that all was quite auspicious.

CHAPTER 11

Sam sat in the dining room of his chosen lodgings, late next morning. It was Sunday. Victoria was no longer with him; he had returned at one o'clock that morning, for they had not gone straight home after the opera. They had wanted to find somewhere for supper and had searched around for somewhere respectable, but in the vicinity there were only establishments with jangling pianos and dancing. They had finally ended up outside the supper room near the Haymarket into which Sam had strayed earlier, now dimly lit with candles and gas lighting; but as soon as they entered, the proprietor had approached them immediately and told them without any apology that under no circumstances were women admitted.

Outside in the street again, Sam had suggested they look further down the Haymarket, but Victoria had said that she did not wish to be home at a ridiculous hour, and in any case the air was becoming uncommonly cold; so Sam had deposited her in the first Hansom that he could conjure up; there appeared to be no other means of transport available, and Victoria was quite enthralled by the idea of travelling by Hansom, despite what others might think of her. "I shall request the driver to put me off at the top of the road where I live," she had said.

"That way father will not see me returning home in such a style. Although I doubt that he has even noticed my absence this evening. I rarely see him after seven o'clock." And she had hopped into the cab, which had shot off immediately along the Hampstead Road, lit up all the way. Sam wondered how the evening had gone. Well, it had not gone badly, therefore it was possible that it had gone well. There was no reason why he could not invite her out again. At least, no romantic reason.

I really do need more money, thought Sam, if I am to maintain the lifestyle to which I have lead Victoria to believe that I am accustomed. Sixty pounds will not go far if I am to spend it on London pleasures. It never occurred to me that Victoria would be so expensive. Thoughts of the square mile and Mr Power were coming back to him as he spread more butter on the large, roughly cut piece of toast that lay before him. I suppose I shall have to become a professional investor. What was that publication that Mr Power had mentioned? The Mining Journal, available from bookstalls and railway stations. Well, Euston Station was just around the corner. I shall do my own investigating this time, thought Sam, and not rely on stockbrokers. They do not care if shares go up or down, they get their money all the same. Straight after breakfast he headed out of his lodgings and was very soon walking along the New Road, now deserted and desolate, towards Drummond Street, where people became visible again, converging towards the great arch of the London and Birmingham Railway. Sam walked through its four classic towering columns across a courtyard and into a great hall furnished with long balconies and colourful murals giving the building the appearance of an art gallery. It however served as a booking area, with porters manoeuvring goods across the marble floor in a most out of place manner. When he reached the platform for the outgoing trains, he observed the difference between how the upper class and working-class travelled; open trucks for those such as himself, and elegant coaches for the more elevated. He watched as those of rank and status accessed the first class compartments by means of a carriage driven directly onto the platform, while those without money were left to scramble onto their uncomfortable vehicles as best they could. In this way, a minimal level of interaction between the distinct groups of travellers was maintained.

Close by was a newsstand and bookstall plastered with posters and bearing the name of W. H. Smith and Son. They appeared to have the Mining Journal and Commercial and Railway Gazette, as was its full name, printed upon the front page. But after purchasing this, Sam spent a full half hour perusing many of the yellow-backed books neatly arranged out in the bookstall. In an act of rashness, he paid out two shillings for a translation of a French novel set in Paris.

"You've no need to worry," said the attendant, as Sam tentatively handed over the coins. "We don't sell penny dreadfuls or shilling shockers here. You'll be getting something of class to read on your journey."

"I've never heard of W. H. Smith," said Sam.

"He set up his first bookstall here in this station two years ago," said the attendant. "And now he's going strong all over the country."

"Well, that is great for him," said Sam, as he walked off, half-reading the yellowback. It was something to do with artists in Paris, and their models. It looked like it was going to be a captivating read. When he got back to his room, however, he opened the pages of the Mining Journal; spreading them out on the bed he turned to the Prices of Mining Shares.

Perhaps it would not be the wisest of moves to put his money back into his previous investment. His eyes ran quickly down the long column of figures and halted at Wheal Tryphena, now priced at 62 ½. He had sold at 80, had he not? No doubt it could fall still further. Mr Power had warned him as to the fickle nature of the copper mining industry; perhaps he should try something completely different this time. In fact, why invest in an English mine at all? There must be far more profitable mines way out in foreign lands; gold and silver were the thing to invest in, were they not? 'The advices from the Linares mines, both private and official, are of a very encouraging character; and a great number of shares have changed hands,' he read. Well, I shall invest part of my money in Linares, then, he decided immediately. The rest I shall put into Royal Santiago as I like the name. All the foreign mines appeared to be doing well, so it didn't really matter into which he put his money, he was sure. The first thing on Monday morning, he would go immediately to Threadneedle Street to instruct Mr Power. No doubt the man would as usual raise his morbid objections about the possibility of shares falling; it was his job, was it not? He could hardly be blamed for such scaremongering. The formalities should not take too long. All business now having been concluded for the day, he turned again to the yellowback, which lay discarded at the other end of the bed and opened it at the first chapter. A long Sunday or a long train journey, it was all the same; the yellow-back would carry him through. Just as the nearby church bells began to peal out mournfully, he put his feet up on the bed and his head back on the pillow; his thoughts went briefly back to By-The-Way Cottage and the dreary Sundays he had spent there – he could do no worse than that. Opening the book at the beginning again he began to read the first paragraph: it was all low-class districts, cafes, men of books and street women; all rambling and timeless. His thoughts returned to Victoria; they had only been briefly away. Surely it would not be long before he would see her again. Then there was a rapping upon the door.

"Yes?" called out Sam.

"I'm serving up luncheon now."

"I'll be right down," said Sam, jumping up from the bed. This was the life. All he needed now was just a little more money.

"I thought I might not have seen the last of you," said Mr Power.

It was Monday morning. Relaxed and confident, Sam was seated yet again opposite his stockbroker. The paper-littered office was becoming quite familiar to him.

"I need to make some further investments," he said, in reply.

"I gathered as much," said Mr Power.

"I have fifty pounds to invest. I have decided upon Linares Mines and Royal Santiago."

"Really? How did you come to decide upon these particular investments?"

"Oh, I did some investigating."

"Well, I cannot see any immediate problem with either of these mines. Though it is my duty as always to advise you that the value of stock can go down as well as up."

"Yes, I know," said Sam, impatiently. "Would you be able to arrange the investment, or do I need to go to some kind of foreign broker?"

"No. I am quite able to handle the transaction. However, for these particular investments, the entire amount will be immediately required by the dealers."

"That's all right. When will the documentation be ready?" said Sam.

"It can be ready within the hour," said Mr Power. "My clerk will see to it."

"Thank you," said Sam, in eagerness. "I have the money with me. I shall return in one hour." And he left at once, not knowing quite were to go. He went off to the --- inn in Capel Court, to while away the hour – there he sat amongst the jobbers and brokers, drinking his usual. It was a lively, jolly place, with an aura of high finance – a transaction appeared to be going on at one neighbouring table. There was a door at the far end of the tavern which led directly into the Stock Exchange; if you were a member, that was. It really was a good life, to be a stockbroker, he considered. But an even better one to be a successful investor. And that was what he intended to be. It was a shame that he had been unaware of the railway boom; but how could he have known of it, stuck in a foundry in Somersetshire? I was not even aware of the existence of shares, he consoled himself, although I was aware that they were building the Great Western Railway – but the idea that someone like me could have profited from something like that would never have occurred to me. Never mind. Better is late than never. When my capital starts to accumulate, then I can really start investing. I can accumulate indefinitely – there is no limit to how much money I can make – I shall keep on and on investing; though I suppose I could always buy a house; I don't want to rent, like Mr Davenport. If I am to marry Victoria, shall need a good house, the larger, the better, with a grand piano and servants. I cannot expect a woman like Victoria to get her hands dirty in the kitchen; she shall never even need to enter a kitchen; I don't suppose she ever has. An investment of fifty pounds would leave him with only a few pounds in his pocket. Well, it would last a while. And he could always get the money back if the share prices failed to rise; it was not spent money.

The hour was almost up; Sam finished his last beer and went off back to Threadneedle Street. There, Mr Power had done everything as promised.

"It is unusual for someone like you to be investing," he said, as he placed the parchment paper and quill in front of Sam. "Most commendable, I must say."

"I shall return in due course," responded Sam, signing his name in a new, flourishing style. "Thank you for your service." It was all out of his hands. Relieved, he got up and departed from Mr Power's office, nodding to the clerk as he walked out into the street again. His mind turned again to Victoria. He was not really sure if they had or had not agreed to meet again in the Adam and Eve, only that he knew she would be there and that she knew that he knew this. But if he were to appear again and the affluent man in the linen suit was there, well, it was not obvious that he would have the upper hand

140

again. Perhaps it would be better to wait a few days before approaching her again. But as he walked back along the New Road an intense desire to see Victoria without delay gained possession of him; as he came to the doors of the Adam and Eve he walked boldly in and through to the back parlour; she was in there alone, near the back in her usual place. As he came up to her, she almost smiled.

"I hope that the Royal Italian Opera met your expectations," he began.

"It more than met my expectations. It greatly surpassed them," she replied. "I feel very privileged to have attended the opening night. And to think that we were in the presence of the Queen and all her royals. Although I must admit, we did not have a very good view of them. Those in the pit probably had a better view."

"Well, if there are any other opportunities that you are desirous of, I shall be happy to oblige," said Sam. Am I speaking a little too flowery, he immediately questioned himself. But she did not appear perturbed.

"May I sit down?" asked Sam.

"If you so wish," was the immediate reply. Sam wondered where the other man was. He did not dare to ask.

"May I buy you your lunch?" asked Sam. He had five pounds in his pocket.

"Well, that would be very good of you," she said at once. "Charles usually pays for my lunch, but he does not appear to have arrived yet."

"Charles? The man you were with on Saturday?"

"That is correct."

"Well, Charles is not the only man who is willing and able to buy you your lunch. I can buy you all the lunches you require."

"So it would seem."

Victoria was suddenly looking over his shoulder. Sam turned to see a well-groomed man adorned in a top hat and recognisable as Charles, in the parlour and advancing unhesitatingly towards him. But on reaching the table, the man's attentions were directed instead towards Victoria.

"I won't ask you what he is doing here," he said, in a tense, clipped tone. "I shall simply ask you what you are intending to do about him."

"I am not intending to do anything about him," she cried. "He just came in a minute ago and offered to buy me a pie and ale. I had no idea that he was coming."

"That is quite correct," Sam found himself saying. "You're too late today, I'm afraid."

The man in the top hat barely gave him a glance. He appeared temporarily speechless. Sam wondered what was going to happen next.

"I shall leave you to your new acquaintance and return when he is gone," said the man, emphatically. "As gone he will soon undoubtedly be. He will not be able to afford you for long, for I doubt that he is as rich as he would have you believe. You are a financial opportunity to him. Goodbye, Victoria." He walked off. The woman gaped at him as he disappeared out into the street again. She continued to stare for some moments afterwards.

"Well," she said, finally. "I've never heard him talk like that before. He must be quite serious after all."

"Shall we get lunch?" asked Sam. Deftly, he took out a luxuriant five pound note from his wallet and placed it ostentatiously upon the table. "I don't carry change," he said, apologetically. "I hope that they will accept this."

"They will not have any choice," said Victoria, her voice enthusiastic and cheerful.

Sam sat comfortably back in the wooden chair.

"What sort of a house would you like to live in, Victoria?" he asked in a sure and certain tone.

"A house?" Well, I would need a room large enough to accommodate a grand piano. So I suppose that it would have to be a fairly substantial house."

"I thought as much," said Sam. "You don't want your grand piano filling up the whole room. Would it have to come through the window or would the legs come off?"

"Er ... the legs would come off," replied Victoria, hesitatingly. There was a pause. Then she spoke again.

"Charles keeps talking about buying me a house," she went on. "But it never happens. I am not sure that it ever will."

"Well," said Sam. "I am thinking of buying a house in the not too distant future. The only question is, where?"

"Well, not around here," said Victoia. "The area is becoming worse by the minute."

"No, certainly not around here," said Sam. "I think a quiet, affluent area would be best. Or what would you say?"

"A quiet, affluent area would be admirable," was her reply. "Where is that lunch? I really am very hungry."

"I'll go and see to it," said Sam, immediately standing up and heading for the bar counter; but then returned, realizing he had forgotten the five pound note.

"Almost forgot this," he said, smiling at his carelessness with money.

"Don't forget the change," said Victoria.

"I will try not to," said Sam. "Though I do hate the

sound of coins jingling in my pocket." He walked deftly up to the bar counter, commanding attention. A fat, knocked-about looking man in an apron came over to him immediately.

"Two good lunches and two pints of ale, at once, if you please," ordered Sam. "In the back parlour."

"Right away, sir." The man disappeared again. As Sam headed back across the oak floor, he was able to observe Victoria's beautiful profile and serene expression. Exactly how much did houses cost? Far too much. Perhaps there would be somewhere acceptable in London where he could rent. Surely that would be within his reach, or at least, as soon as those shares went up. Somewhere like St John's Wood might be ideal, except that it was too close to the Davenports. He went back to Victoria, carrying the ales.

"How soon were you thinking of moving?" she asked immediately as he sat down again.

"Oh, very soon," said Sam, at once. "It could be a matter of weeks. I was actually thinking of renting rather than buying. It is quite the done thing nowadays."

"I suppose it is. But people of means usually do own at least one property."

"Do they? Well, I suppose many of them do. I am afraid that I am not classifiable as landed gentry."

"I am sure you are quite right to rent. If the house is not to your liking, you can move."

"Oh, I am sure it will be to my liking. I rarely change my mind," said Sam.

"I am glad to hear it," said she.

"As soon as I move, I shall let you know immediately," said Sam, just as the steaming plates of meat pudding were arriving at the table. "Capital," said Sam, as they were placed before him and Victoria. The waiter plonked down some cutlery and walked away.

"The humble pudding," said Sam, picking up the fork. "Eaten by rich and poor alike."

She smiled and said, "I can imagine you fitting in anywhere. Why, I can just as easily see you labouring over a hot furnace as I can see you in shirt sleeves, sitting behind a desk."

"Well I'm afraid that I cannot say the same of you," said Sam. "Under no stretch of my imagination can I see you behind a bar, or carrying milk pails."

"Father is determined that no such fate shall befall me," she said. "That is why he is so concerned about Charles' income."

"I see his point," said Sam. And there was no lie in this statement. "I too shall ensure that no such fate shall befall you."

"Are you really able to do such a thing?"

"Without a doubt. Nothing would prevent me from protecting you from hardship."

"I am most gratified," said she. "But I have heard Charles talk in a similar manner for a long time, and nothing has come of it. Words alone are of no value. I have been told that all things come to those who wait, but I am wondering how long I shall have to wait."

"If you rely on Charles, it could be a very long time," said Sam, sombrely. "He does not strike me as a man of resolution."

"I believe you may be right. If only he were a bit more resolute."

"Though no doubt he has many admirable qualities."

"Yes, I suppose he does."

"Well, you can't have everything."

"I do not seem able to have anything, just now."

"You have more than most. Not that I would know about the misery of poverty."

"It is poverty that I fear most. My father's resources are limited. I could be heading in the direction of the workhouse."

"It will not happen," responded Sam. "I shall make sure of it."

"Yes, I know," she said, wearily. "That is what Charles is always saying."

CHAPTER 12

It was with eagerness and optimism that Sam walked into the grand hall of Euston Station the following Sunday and onto the familiar departure platform. How were his shares doing? Perhaps it was a little too soon to hope for any change. As he purchased the Mining Journal he was greeted again by the same attendant who had been there last time - he seemed to Sam to be abnormally content with his work.

"How did you get on with the book?" the man asked, drinking out of a beaker something that looked like coffee. Sam wondered if it was palatable.

"Oh, I got on pretty well," said Sam. "Got through several chapters, at least. I don't do much reading."

He did not wait to get back to his room, but walked back along the platform, trying to find the relevant page. When he found it, his reaction was not altogether positive. He had bought shares in Royal Santiago at 13 ½ pence. They were now at 11 ¼. He looked up away from the newspaper as he continued to walk on back through the hall, into the courtyard and through the great arch. Well, no doubt they would soon recover. It was probably just a temporary aberration. There would be no point in instructing Mr Power to sell now, and then watch them go up again. Linares were still stable at 3 ½ pence a share.

Perhaps I should have bought shares in a wide range of companies, he considered; some might go up, some might go down. Maybe that was a safer approach. But it was too late now, he felt. He would just wait for the shares in Royal Santiago to go up again. After all, he had not yet lost very much money; a mere fifteen percent of it or thereabouts. But it was not in a joyous state that he returned to his lodgings, passing the Adam and Eve on the way, and briefly looking in to check that Victoria was not there, as he knew she would not be, on a Sunday. Well, it must not be with a dimmed look that I come in here to see Victoria tomorrow, he told himself. Victoria would dismiss me instantly in favour of that other man, should she discern my true financial state. And he quickened his pace once more, pretending to himself that the shares in Royal Santiago had in fact gone up, not down. To regain his power, once through the door of his lodgings, he insisted on paying Mrs --- another four weeks in advance.

"I have never had a lodger such as you," she said, in a most gratified tone, accepting the money without any hesitation. "You're quite ideal."

Sam smiled briefly and returned to his room. He opened out the mine shares pages again and observed that most of the shares had not moved in their value at all. Well, I wanted something that was actually going to move, he reflected. The only problem was, those that he had chosen had moved in the wrong direction. Listlessly, he picked up the yellowback that was lying on the window sill beside the bed. I don't really think I can be bothered to finish this, he decided. Reading was a little bit too much like hard work.

There was always next Sunday, he consoled himself.

Next Sunday he would return to Euston Station, and everything would have righted itself again. He put the matter out of his mind and lolled back on the bed, musing over what he would say to Victoria the following day. Then considering his suit a little dusty, he went back downstairs to find out if Mrs --- had such a thing as a clothes brush. His hair could also do with a cut. He would go to the hairdresser on the New Road tomorrow morning, before going to the Adam and Eve. The coarse, mournful church bell rang out in the not too far distance; it went on for at least half an hour as it always did on Sundays. Everything will be all right when Victoria and I are married, he concluded, throwing off any anxiety that he might be feeling. It is not where you are, it is where you are going. The hours dragged on into the late afternoon, evening and night; a long night but eventually it was the next day, and he was walking along the New Road at noon, in a somewhat refreshed, new state; neat, clean and with a recent haircut. When he entered the back parlour of the Adam and Eve, he saw Victoria in the presence of two men dressed in working clothes, who apparently wished to annoy her. One had a jug of ale in one hand and one foot on the chair opposite, whilst the other stood over her. "You don't have any problem with us, do you?" he was asking. Sam walked up to the table.

"If you do not mind, gentlemen," he began, putting an emphasis on the word, 'gentlemen', "but I would very much prefer it if you would go back to your business and leave this woman alone."

After a pause, they sloped off without a word or grimace.

"I hope you are all right," said Sam, when they were out of the parlour.

"Yes, thank you," said Victoria, apparently only slightly perturbed. "It has happened before. It is so difficult to find somewhere to eat, especially around here."

"Yes, I can imagine," said Sam. "It is quite disgraceful that a respectable woman cannot find a tavern these days."

Victoria seemed briefly to notice his new, improved presentation, with a fairly positive reaction. Sam sat down opposite her. A plate of meat lay before her, and she began to eat again.

"How is everything, Victoria?" he went on.

"Oh, quite all right, thank you," she said. "Although I did have a rather tedious weekend. Nothing to do, really, except practice."

"Oh! Well, I thought perhaps we might take a boat trip along the Thames next weekend," said Sam immediately. "All the way to Hampton Court." But she did not light up as he had hoped she would.

"Oh, I would love to," she said. "I went once before, and it was most pleasant. But Charles wishes me to accompany him to a dinner party. He does not want to go alone – he feels that he will make a better impression with me at his side. They are people of elevated rank – it is not often that he receives such an invitation. I really cannot refuse."

"Oh," said Sam. He remembered the Davenports. Well, they were not really people of elevated rank, but they had something going for them.

"I have been present at a few dinner parties since arriving in London," he said. "In St John's Wood. The houses there are large, but not grand."

"The house to which we are invited is situated in May Fair," said Victoria. "I know very little about St John's Wood. Is it a fashionable area?"

"It depends what sort of fashion you are looking for," said Sam. "I don't think it would suit you."

"Oh, all sorts of things suit me," said Victoria. Sam's heart rose again. But then she said, "Charles is thinking of entering the legal profession."

"Why is he doing that?" asked Sam.

"To increase his income, of course. He is permanently caught in the trap of neither having to work nor enjoying a life of affluence."

"Will it be easy for him to enter the legal profession?"

"No, but there is a possibility."

Sam suppressed a sigh. "Well, that should keep him busy," he said, finally.

"Are you hoping to continue in your former profession?" asked Victoria. "Or find a new one?"

"No, I am not," said Sam. "I am quite happy to continue to enjoy a life of affluence. Would you like anymore to eat?"

"No, thank you," said Victoria. "I have to go back to the office. But thank you for your invitation to go on the boat trip. Maybe the weekend after next, I shall be free."

"Shall I walk back with you?"

"Yes, why ever not."

As they got up to leave and walked out into the street together, there was no sign of Charles hanging about anywhere. It would be years before the man qualified as a lawyer. My shares will have gone through the roof by then, thought Sam, reassuringly.

*

On Saturday, Sam thought of Victoria, dressing in front of a mirror, meticulously preparing herself for Charles' important dinner party. He hoped that it would all go wrong; perhaps if Victoria did not behave conventionally, Charles would decide that she was an unsuitable match for him. She would almost certainly play for them on the grand piano in the drawing room; perhaps she would make an unfortunate choice of music and upset them all. This week's Mining Journal would already be out, he was sure, for it was always dated for the Saturday. After Mrs --- 's generous breakfast, he was straight down to the Doric Arch of Euston Station again, welcoming the sight of the bustle in the great hall; he walked onto the smoky platform and admired the ironwork above. The attendant was there as usual, with his beaker of coffee on a stool beside him.

"Mining Journal?" he enquired, taking out one of the three on the rack.

"Yes," said Sam. "Is the coffee here drinkable?"

"That is a matter of opinion," said he. "But I've been drinking it for two years, and it hasn't killed me yet. How about another novel? You won't get the same novel cheaper anywhere else."

"No, thanks," said Sam. "I find reading rather difficult. I prefer the theatre."

Back in the Great Hall, he leant against the archway columns, thumbing restlessly through the pages. But on finding the mining share prices, it was the case that shares in Royal Santiago now stood at 8½ pence – a drop in 2½ pence per share. Linares were now at 2¾; a drop in ¼ of a pence per share. Sam did not want to calculate how much money that left him with; one thing was clear:

he must go directly to Mr Power on Monday and get his money out of these losing shares. I shall put them into something else, he thought, resolutely. Mr Power will be able to advise me, as he did last time with the copper mining shares. I should have asked him to do so in the first place. He must have a better idea than I do as to which shares will rise and which will fall. Well, no doubt he can get me out of the fix. I just wish it were already Monday – now it will be a full day and a half before I may consult him. What to do for a day and a half. The public-houses opened at noon. That was five minutes ago. He wondered out of the station again, back into the New Road, and walked away from the Adam and Eve quite a distance, past the Marylebone workhouse and eventually into a pub called the Green Man.

Inside was a large bar counter, accessible from all sides, which extended right, left and forwards into the other rooms. It was already surrounded by men who most likely had been in there all morning. "Good day," he said cheerfully to the one standing beside him, as he ordered and was served very quickly. He was home again and could forget anything that irked him. The man beside him professed to be a builder named Higgs. He lived next door and had never been married. He drank there whenever he was able to, which was every working day from dusk until the small hours, and much of the week-end. Eventually, Higgs went to sit down in one of the back rooms leaving Sam standing at the bar. He ordered another, then another, wondering how he could have done without drink for so long. And as he continued to drink, he became ever more convinced that he could assuredly leave all his financial affairs in the safe hands of Mr Power.

At nine-thirty on Monday morning, the clerk of John Power, stockbroker, was shuffling up to his employer's office in Threadneedle Street, to tiredly unlock the door and let himself into the dim interior of the reception area. No sooner was he within when Sam appeared at the doorway, in an apparent state of unrest. The clerk watched as this young man stepped awkwardly into the office.

"Could I make an appointment to see Mr Power as soon as possible," said Sam, in a virtual gasp.

The clerk looked absently towards him. "He's not here yet," he responded. Then he slowly opened the small, black book and thumbed through the pages.

"I should think he can see you when he comes in."

"Then I shall wait here," said Sam, sitting down immediately in one of the leather backed upright chairs in the reception. The clerk coughed and sat down at his own desk. He then proceeded to do nothing.

"Got some urgent business to attend to?" he said, presently.

"Yes. At what time does the Stock Exchange open?" asked Sam.

"Eleven o'clock."

"So late?"

"They open later on Monday morning."

"Well, then I should be all right," said Sam. "I suppose that shares cannot move in value too much in ten minutes."

"Well, they can actually," said the drab, unambitious man. "What with the telegraph."

"Telegraph?"

"It's a new invention. London is linked up to all the major cities with it. The London Stock Exchange receives share prices from the Edinburgh Stock Exchange in less than five minutes."

"Really? What about foreign share prices?"

"Oh, that could take two weeks. But it won't be long before the whole world is wired up."

Mr Power was stepping in. His eyes darted briefly at Sam and then to his clerk.

"Mr Brazenall wishes to consult with you as soon as is convenient," said the clerk.

"Now's as good a time as any. Step this way, Mr Brazenall," said Mr Power, wasting no time in walking into his office beyond. Sam followed him apprehensively. As soon as they were settled inside, he began at once to tell Mr Power of his predicament. Mr Power continued to listen until Sam stopped talking. Sam waited for his response.

"I am not sure that I would advocate selling at this point in time," said Mr Power, surprisingly. "It is likely that in the long term, the shares will return to their original value."

"In the long term?" repeated Sam. "I haven't got long. I've already lost half of them already. I want them saved now so that I can put them into something better."

"Such as?" queried Mr Power.

"Well, I was hoping that you would be able to advise me on that."

"I have already given my advice. Hold on to the shares."

"I don't think that I can do that," said Sam. He picked up the copy of the Mining Journal which he had brought with him and placed on the table. "I seem to have done particularly badly. Most of the other mines seem to have been all right."

"Well, you were lucky to break into profit so soon with your first shares," said Mr Power. "And now the luck has been compensated by a piece of bad luck."

"How about Barossa Range?"

"Barossa Range is as good as any."

"In that case, sell my shares in Royal Santiago and Linares and put three-quarters of the money into Barossa Range."

"Certainly," said Mr Power. "Though it is my duty to remind you that these shares may also fall."

"Yes, I know," said Sam. "Shall I come back in an hour?"

"No. If you would just sign an application for the shares now, I shall arrange everything at the earliest possible opportunity."

"Shall I come back for the share certificate?"

"If you like. Alternatively, I can keep it safe for you."

"Oh, yes, that might be better," said Sam. "I would prefer for you to keep hold of it."

"Very well, then," said Mr Power, reaching for his exquisitely made quill and then writing, this time more slowly than usual. Eventually, he proffered the quill and parchment to Sam, who took them from him. As he signed, Mr Power looked on, as though he was still quite baffled and surprised that this client could write.

"There you are," said Sam.

"Thank you. No doubt I shall be seeing you again in due course."

"Definitely," said Sam.

"Well, good day to you then," said Mr Power, getting up from the desk. Sam did the same and left the office at once. He did not even look at the clerk in the entrance area but hurried out into the street, heading straight for the nearest public-house. It is quite amazing just how fast shares can go up or down, he reflected, as he began to drink again with no end to the drinking in sight. No doubt they will be up again by next week, and the nightmare will be over. I can't be unlucky three weeks running. He decided to put the matter out of his mind so that next Saturday he would be as cool and calm as possible; for otherwise Victoria might notice his anxious expression and deduce that things were not as they should be.

The following Saturday Sam really was on a boat to Hampton Court, with Victoria. They had boarded at Hungerford and now stood at the front of the steamer, amongst a mixed class of people. Victoria was wearing a wide-brimmed hat and white gloves. From the other end of the boat came the strains of a waltz played on quaint wind instruments; the band of musicians appeared to have been let on free of charge, and no doubt would be handing around a collection cap. But despite all these diversions, Victoria did not seem to be entirely amused. She was not conversing easily with him but continued to stare out along the river.

"Is anything wrong, Victoria?" Sam finally ventured to ask.

"No, nothing," she replied. But then a little later she turned to him and said,

"You seem a little disappointed, Sam. A bit sad and dusty."

"Yes, I am," admitted Sam. "The stock market has lost some of its value. Some of my shares were hit."

"Oh, dear," she said. "That is not good news at all."

"But I have rearranged my investments," added Sam hastily. "I am sure it is only a temporary setback."

"A temporary setback?" echoed Victoria. Her tone was not altogether approving.

"These things happen even to the most astute of investors," said Sam. "It is all in a day's work. It is not a matter that I would wish to bore you with."

"I am always most interested in your business affairs," said Victoria. "Which areas do you invest in?"

"Oh, the mining sector, mainly. Foreign mines in particular. At the moment I am specialising in copper and silver."

"Oh. Are they reliable commodities?"

"Well, not really. They are both fickle. Especially copper. But they may yield a richer return than some of the more reliable commodities."

"I suppose that is what they call, speculation."

"Yes. You have to speculate to accumulate."

"You have a need to accumulate?"

"Most definitely. I intend to become one of the richest men in England."

"Well, I hope your investments recover soon," she said, staring out again along the Thames. "It would be very annoying if they were wiped out. You would have to return to your uninviting work."

"Do not contemplate such a thing," said Sam. "I do not believe that it will happen."

"I sincerely hope that it will not."

They were being propelled along faster; Sam could see

the tide swirling in. He pointed out a couple of swans and their cygnets on the bank. It was a while since he had seen such sights.

"You would like Somerset," he said, in a more relaxed tone. "It was not until I left the area that I realized how picturesque it was there. Yet I was not happy there."

"Do you have a house in Somerset?"

"Only the family house," he said.

"Do you not ever get tired of renting lodgings?"

"All the time," said Sam. "But I am not yet settled."

"I must confess I am tired of residing in my father's house," said she. "But in my present circumstances, there would appear to be no alternative."

Sam wished that he had a house. "I shall look into the idea of renting a house directly," he said finally. "You are right. One cannot stay in lodgings forever. Just as one cannot remain a bachelor forever."

"I cannot see myself as a spinster forever," said Victoria. "The idea is too tragic even to think about."

"Have no fear," said Sam. "The situation will resolve itself very soon."

"So Charles keeps telling me."

Sam turned to her. "Perhaps Charles is not the man for you," he intimated. "In any case, it might be ill-advised to put all your eggs in one basket."

"They are not really in any basket," said Victoria. "When exactly are you planning to move into a house?"

"As soon as possible."

"Will the house be in that place you mention ... St John's Wood?"

"I don't think so," said Sam. "There are people there that I do not wish to meet accidentally."

"Oh," said Victoria. "That's a shame. It sounded like a rather colourful area."

"That is precisely the reason why I doubt if your father would approve of you living there."

"Oh, as long as I were financially secure, he would not care where I lived."

"I shall make some immediate enquiries," said Sam. After all, anyone could make enquiries. When he had the money, the enquiries could be acted upon; and it was clear that once he had a house, he would have Victoria. All she seemed to want in the world was a house.

Victoria spoke again. "I thought that you were already making enquiries," she said.

"No, I have not really got around to it."

"Why not?"

"Well, I have only just retired from my profession. I have hardly had time to think about it."

"It all sounds a bit strange," said Victoria. "I do not find you greatly forthcoming."

"Don't you?" said Sam, nervously. The pause that followed only served to increase his awkwardness.

"Are you sure that you can afford to rent a house?" asked Victoria, suddenly turning to look at him with a critical expression. "They can be very expensive, especially in the more affluent areas of London."

"For you, Victoria, I can afford anything."

She turned her head away. Up in the distance, the red brick towers of Hampton Court were looming above the trees beyond. "I see that we are nearly at the palace," he observed, lamely.

"Yes, but I would prefer if we did not alight there,"

said Victoria. "Let us remain on the boat for the return journey to London."

"I thought you wanted to see the palace,"

"Well, I have changed my mind. I have, after all, seen it once before, and it is really rather dreary. Also, I do not wish to be back too late. My father will object."

"As you wish, Victoria," said Sam, dejectedly. As the boat chugged, on he tried to think of something interesting to say, but could not. Victoria apparently had nothing to say either; however, when the boat finally docked at Hampton Court, and everyone save them filed off to be guided to the palace, she said, "This is like a school outing."

The boat wasted no time in collecting the waiting passengers and reversing direction. To his disbelief, Sam saw that the last passenger to board was almost thrown into the Thames, so abrupt was the departure.

"I hear there are almost daily collisions between boats on the Thames," said Sam.

"I believe so. Ideally, I would not now be standing on this steamer," said Victoria.

Sam suppressed a sigh; it was going to be a long journey home. Perhaps no conversation was better than antagonistic conversation. He decided to leave Victoria to her bitter and suspicious thoughts and became aware of the continual chugging of the steamer and the loose chatter around them. Interesting species of birds seemed to be colonising the banks of the river. He began to think of Somerset; of its gently rolling landscape and clear air. Were there no flax mill or foundry there, it would not be such a bad place. From the perspective of a mill owner, there really was nothing wrong with the place at all.

CHAPTER 13

On Sunday morning, the following day, Sam lay on his bed in his lodgings, staring at the unchanging figure of two pence a share in the South Australian copper mine that he had so carefully invested in. At the same time he reflected upon the day before, spent in Victoria's lukewarm company. Had she guessed that he was not a member of the idle rich, as she had previously supposed, but was in fact a member of the idle poor? He would have to start renting an impressive residence; that would allay any fears that she might have. But first, he would need to raise the money. Barossa Range was not performing as it should. Agitatedly, he threw the paper aside. Was there no quick way of making money? Charles was winning. The man had a guaranteed thousand pounds and was trying to better himself by becoming a member of the professions. Well, any 'profession' that was available to me would not result in me winning Victoria, thought Sam. So I may as well not bother. Finally, he decided to calculate mentally how much money he now had in the world came to roughly twenty-nine pounds. That included the small amount released from the last share transaction, for living expenses and Victoria. That money would soon go; then he would be forced to release more money.

Did Victoria even want to see him again? He was

not sure. The day before they had parted on reasonably amicable terms. There would be no harm in approaching her one more time, to see if she was still in the same mood. But perhaps it would be better to wait a while. This, however, he found impossible, and the following afternoon he saw Victoria in the Adam and Eve as usual, and although he was quite careful not to mention them, she seemed strangely aware of his troubles. Charles continued to be absent.

"How are your stocks and shares doing?" she asked, cordially.

"My stocks and shares? Oh, they have fallen again slightly," said Sam. "But I am sure they must soon turn."

"Well, I can only wish the best for you," said Victoria. Then, filling in the silence that followed, she went on, "Charles is to study law at University College London. His uncle has agreed to pay the fees."

"How much are the fees?"

"Twenty pounds per annum."

"Oh," said Sam. "That's not too bad."

"Then there are his living expenses. He will be living in the college residences."

"Has his uncle agreed to pay for that, too?"

"Yes. All Charles has to do now is work hard."

"He won't have much time for you, then."

"Oh, I don't mind, as long as it leads to an elevation of his status."

"Well, in the mean time whilst Charles is slogging I'm sure we shall have great fun, going on boat trips and other excursions," said Sam.

"If you can afford it," said Victoria, suddenly looking anxious.

"Yes," said Sam. He kept imagining Charles walking into the public-house in his cap and gown. "Perhaps I should have been a banker."

"Only titled men become bankers," said Victoria. "Charles could never become a banker."

"Yes, I suppose he would have to settle for a more intermediate position in the banking hierarchy," agreed Sam wholeheartedly.

"Charles has no intention of becoming a bank clerk."

"No, I'm sure he doesn't," agreed Sam. He did not wish to talk about Charles.

"Do you have anything planned for next weekend, Victoria?" he asked, hopefully.

"Next Saturday I am fully occupied."

"Oh," said Sam. "Well, how about Sunday, then? Or the weekend after? Or whenever you are next free? Is there anything you would like to do?"

"I will have to see. Charles may be needing me."

"Do you wish to dispense of me, Victoria?"

For a moment, she did not speak.

"I think perhaps we should not go on any more outings for a while," she said, finally. "Until you are more financially settled."

"Whatever you say, Victoria," said Sam, trying not to look too glum. "I think I had better go, now."

"Stay if you wish."

"I do not think that there is any point in me staying," said Sam, without reproach. "Charles may be arriving soon, and no doubt he has much to tell you. A lawyer's life can be nothing but glamour and excitement."

"Whatever you wish," she said, indifferently. Sam decided to leave; and as he did, he was unsurprised to see

Charles approaching from the opposite side of the street, with a determined and business-like step, with which he was sure he could not compete. With quiet resignation, he retreated to his lodgings, whereupon he counted out his remaining coins, grateful that he had not paid out for Victoria's lunch today.

When Saturday came round, and Sam was in the station again, he was ready for the final blow. He had bought the latest copy of the Mining Journal, ruing the expense and was sitting in the refreshment room. The coffee was as bad as it was reputed to be and the sandwiches had been made yesterday. Barossa Range had fallen to ¾ of a pence per share. That, he calculated instantly, left him with the princely sum of ten pounds. Not much more than he had started out with, two years ago. The sound of a steam whistle as a train departed from the platform made him wish he was on it; then he realized that he had nowhere to go. He walked out of the refreshment room, through the grandiose Great Hall of Euston Station and back to his lodgings, trooping dejectedly up the three flights of stairs and into his shilling room. He glanced miserably around. The chair, iron bedstead and clothes box, although Spartan and functional, now seemed like luxury. In two weeks or so, he would be back in the low lodging-houses. His privacy would be gone – and he would once again be forced to mix with the most unsavoury types of characters. First it would be the fourpenny lodging-houses, then the threepenny lodging-houses, then the workhouses, and finally, when winter came round again, the Asylum for the Homeless in Cripplegate. Once again, he thought of writing to his mother. She had answered his first letter; he could write to her again. At least I can write my own letter, he thought, proudly. I do not have to pay a letter writer. Not having pen or ink, he went out to the Post Office Receiving House that was just along the New Road to write it. It was a long time since he had written anything. The premises of the Receiving House were that of a tradesman, and for a halfpenny, the woman there gave him a scrap of paper and the use of a quill. He stood at the far end of the counter, writing.

Dear mother, he began. But after that, he could not think of anything else to write. He placed the quill down. Then it occurred to him that maybe his mother had already written to him sometime during the last year. Having nowhere else to send it, she would have sent it to this post office. He looked up at the woman and came over to the till where she was standing.

"Are there any letters for me?" he asked, pessimistically.

"What is your name?"

"Samuel Brazenall."

She disappeared, then returned very quickly with a letter, handing it at once to Sam. The writing on the envelope was at once recognisable as his mother's.

"Thank you," said Sam. He took it out of the building and stood outside in the street, reading it.

Dear Sam

I hope you are well and are now working again.
I have to give you the sad news that your father
has died. He died suddenly last week at work. We
have very little money now. I am not sure how we

are going to manage. I am trying my best to be economical.

Daniel has left home. He married Margery from The Red Lion six months ago. She is expecting a child in June. He needs all the money he can earn and cannot spare much for us. There are only eleven of us in the house now.

Mother

P.S. We have cut down the tree in the garden as it was a hazard during gales.

It was time to go home. Now he could not wait to return to By-The-Way Cottage, from which he should never have strayed, at least, not without more thought and preparation. He walked quickly back along the New Road and down the side street, not regretting that he would forgo the pleasures of renewing the communal life of the low lodging-houses of London; the exchanging of stories and anecdotes with its jolly inmates and the readings of such volumes as Dick Turpin and Jonathan Wild. Not that he had ever really enjoyed the supposed gaiety, despite the bewildering exuberance of the others. In less than three weeks he would have reached the Somerset border. He could already visualize the hazy, extensive view across Dorset; no longer did it seem over familiar. He would leave as soon as all had been attended to: a final visit to Mr Power, and the retrieval of two weeks' deposit from Mrs ---. She was surely the only person in London who would miss him. "So you're leaving," he imagined her saying; "I'm so sorry to see you go. You've been a wonderful lodger."

But when he did speak to her, she seemed strangely

uninterested. He stopped her in the hallway of the boarding-house, where she was sweeping. She did not seem to take it in to start with.

"Leaving, are you?"

"Yes, I'm afraid so. I would, however, like to tell you that I have been quite happy here."

"I'm glad to hear it."

"I wonder if I could trouble you for the return of my deposit."

"Oh." She seemed put out. "You'll have to wait a couple of days for that. I don't keep a lot of cash in the house."

"I don't have a couple of days," said Sam. "I wish to leave London immediately."

"Well then, I'm afraid I really can't help you," said Mrs ---, beginning to sweep again. "In any case, when I was cleaning your room yesterday I noticed rather a large tear in the curtain. It needs replacing."

"It was torn when I moved in."

"I didn't notice," said Mrs ---. "You should have told me then."

"Oh, forget it," said Sam. "I do not have time for those such as you." He went back up to the room to pack his bag. Now he really did want to leave at once. He glanced at the curtain. Mrs ... was right. The tear that he had been vaguely aware of had become bigger. He immediately took down the curtain. Stuffing it in his bag together with his other few things, he threw the key on to the dressing table and hurried out, clumping noisily down the stairs again. Mrs --- was no longer in the hallway. Once out in the street, he headed in a westerly direction along the New Road, past the Marylebone Workhouse, continuing on until he reached the Uxbridge Road, which took him out of the great capital city with amazing rapidity. He passed the Halfway Hotel Public-house and was told that the London to Banbury coach stopped there; but it seemed quicker and easier to keep on walking. As the houses gave way to fields, market gardens and allotments, he knew that he had left London behind and was en route to home.

CHAPTER 14

Sam trudged along the London Road, towards Bourton and Leigh Common. Everything around him was familiar again. The thought of his father's rantings kept returning; he had to keep reminding himself that his father was gone and that the house would now be quiet. Now he would be welcome at home. Daniel would not be there either, leaving the room upstairs all for his own personal use. He wondered how his mother would react when she saw him. She would never turn him away, he was sure. As the eldest son, he would now be the head of household. That also meant that he would be expected to be the main earner. As he approached Factory Hill, he glanced upwards towards the chimneys of the foundry, smoking into the clear sky. In a week or so, he would be back in there, that was if they would take him. Without his father's help, it would be harder to persuade Messrs. Maggs and Co. to put him on their books again.

Coming up to the rise out of Bourton, Sam reached The Red Lion. It was, as always, lit up, jolly and inviting. But Sam did not go in. He continued on resolutely, anxious not to delay his home arrival by a single minute. In the twilight, he covered the final undulating two miles in view of the hazy, peaceful landscape. Down the slope he went, past The Hunter's Lodge, until he was standing before the verdant archway to the path leading up to By-The-Way Cottage. The door was shut, and nobody was in the garden. But there were signs that the grass had recently been attended to. The curtains at the windows were drawn aside and Sam caught sight of two unfamiliar faces watching him from upstairs. He walked down the path. It was not necessary for him to knock at the door, for it opened to reveal a brother, suddenly far more grown up than Sam had remembered him from a year ago.

"It's Sam," proclaimed the boy. "He's back, mother."

Sam's mother appeared in the light hallway, carrying a tea-towel. "Sam," she said. "I never thought that I would see you again."

"And nor I you, mother," said Sam. "I received your letter. I thought you might want your eldest son back at home again."

"It was not me who turned you away, before," said his mother. "I could not go against your father's wishes."

"No, mother, I know," said Sam. "Though now I realise that father was not all bad. He simply felt that I could survive alone if I truly wished to."

"Oh, Sam, in the past I did wish that you could learn to work," said his mother. "But now I am glad just to see you here at all. You can never really take your father's place but are still a blessing to me. Come through, we are about to eat our dinner."

With relief, Sam stepped into the parlour. All his brothers and sisters were somewhere about; the two youngest ones were no longer infants; they sat dignifiedly upon the chairs at the table. His eldest sister was now advanced enough to be classified as a woman and was quietly helping to lay out the table. Without any consideration for his appearance, Sam took his old place at one end of the table, relishing the thought of a good meal to come.

"So, Daniel is now married to Marge," he said, as he waited for the plate laden with meat and potatoes to appear miraculously before him.

"Yes, that's right. I am glad for him. It is healthier to be married."

"I'd have thought he could have done better than Marge."

"Just because you can not see Margery's virtues, that does not mean she has none," said his mother, from the sink. "She is now your sister-in-law, and I would like you to regard her as such."

"Yes, mother, but Marge ..."

"I will hear no disrespectful talk of Margery," said his mother. Sam was quiet; if Daniel was stupid enough to marry Marge, that was his affair. He began to eat; the food seemed more real than any food that he had had for some time.

"What will you do now that you are back here, Sam?" asked his mother, when he had finished the meal. She came over to take the plate away.

"I shall seek work in the foundry again," said Sam. "Though without father's recommendation, it could be difficult to regain any kind of position."

"I shall speak to the Reverend," said his mother, assuredly. "I am sure he can help."

"I don't think that doddery old vicar is capable of making anything happen," said Sam. "They won't listen to him."

"I am referring to the vicar of Bourton," said his

mother. "Not the one of Stoke Trister. The vicar of Bourton is a good friend of the Maggs, and fully aware of my precarious situation. I am sure he will persuade them to take you on in some capacity."

"In some capacity?"

"Beggars can not be choosers," said his mother.

"There must be another way to live," said Sam, determinedly. "Why, I have heard of many people emigrating to the New World, where they are given land to work on. The land is theirs if they are the first to claim it."

"You would not like that, Sam," said his mother. "Working the land would be harder than work at the foundry."

"Well, at least I would not be in prison. I would have no overseer."

"You would find it a prison none-the-less. The land itself would be your overseer."

"There must be a way out," said Sam. "It cannot be 'work or starve.' There are people who started with nothing and ended with everything."

"Who are these people?"

"While living in the lodging-houses of London, I heard tales read aloud from books, written by great authors. In these, there are men who were convicts and then became millionaires in Australia. And coster-girls who become actresses. We are living in a new age. Anything is possible."

"That is fantasy," observed his mother. "In reality, it would not work. Nothing like that will work, except for possibly, prostitution."

"This I do not believe," said Sam. "It cannot be so."

"You have seen for yourself that you must work,"

insisted his mother, now back in the kitchen. "For more than a year, you have lived as a vagabond. You have no money. And with your father gone, we need every penny. The little money that he had saved for us will soon be gone."

"I had money," said Sam, defiantly. "For a little while."

His mother turned abruptly towards him. "What do you mean, Sam?" she asked.

"Just that," went on Sam, ruefully. "I was once almost rich enough to get on. But I made a bad investment and lost it all again. It was not quite enough, you see ... I just needed a little more; if I had had twice as much, it would have sufficed. So I tried to double my money, but lost nearly all."

"I will not ask you how you obtained the money in the first place," said his mother. "But as I am sure it was not honourably come by, to lose it was no tragedy. You must learn to earn money, Sam, not merely to gain it."

"I shall try again," said Sam. "If I just had a little capital."

"Only the rich have capital," said his mother. "That is something you cannot think of. Instead, you should think of the solid, steady income that you would have had if you had not gone astray."

"A life of drudgery," said Sam. "I am no slave, mother."

"Then I shall starve with you, Sam," said his mother. "For in a month, all the money will be gone. We shall have to ask for assistance from the Poor Fund."

Sam sighed. "I shall return to the foundry," he said. "For a little while."

*

The following evening Sam headed up the hill from Leigh Common towards Bourton. He had spent the day in idleness; he was glad that there was no point in his approaching the foundry foreman in person. Walking towards The Red Lion always seemed like a much shorter walk than walking away from it, despite the longer uphill stretches. In the twilight, it struck him how pleasing the scenery was to the eye – quite picturesque. He finally came over the last hill and up to the welcome façade of The Red Lion, with its verdant vegetation sprawling around it, and lamplight emanating invitingly from within. Taking a furtive glance behind him, he stepped inside for the first time in over a year. Apart from the absence of Marge, nothing had changed. In the glow of an oil lamp, he could see that his usual bench by the window opposite was unoccupied, as though awaiting his return. In a few minutes, the men would be pouring in. Tomorrow, he might be one of them again. He sat down.

An unfamiliar barmaid of voluptuous proportions appeared beside him. "I ain't seen you in 'ere before, 'ave I?"

"No, I don't believe you have." She was an improvement on Marge, but nothing to shout about. "I drink beer," he announced, somewhat curtly. All the old familiarities of the place were returning to him. The maid moved off. Sam looked casually around him; the men were starting to fill up the place. He did not recognise all of them. Thomas Dawes from the flax mill abruptly entered the premises; on seeing Sam, he stopped melodramatically dead in his tracks.

"Yes, it is I," said Sam. "You are not drunk yet."

Tom walked up to him. "Wales not to your liking?" he enquired.

"You've got a good memory," said Sam. "Well, I didn't stay there long; I only went there to see life. And that I did. Then I moved on to London."

"London? You must have done well there," said Tom. "The streets are paved with gold."

"They're paved with stone, as you might expect," said Sam. "And those who live on them have a hard time of it, I can tell you, especially in the winter. There's no help for those without shelter except the asylums, and they're terrible places."

"You don't say."

"I do. One summer and one winter I spent there, with nothing to eat but a stale crust or two. After that I had mixed fortune, ending in bankruptcy. Then mother wrote to tell me that father had died. So I knew I would finally be welcome back at home. So here I am."

The barmaid appeared again, carrying a tray laden with beers. "The usual?" she enquired of Tom.

"Yes, Queenie," said Tom. He stared after her as she swayed back to the bar. Sam looked at him sarcastically. Tom recovered himself. "Where will you be working?" he enquired, critically. "I doubt if you'll want to show your face again, back at the foundry."

"Why not?"

"Well, you're not exactly sought after material, are you? Anyway, they're full up."

"Well, I shall have to try the flax mill, then," said Sam.

"Not a chance," said Tom.

"Well, then I suppose I'm back on the road again, tomorrow," said Sam. "I just came here for a visit really, to see how everyone was getting on."

"I'd say the future looks very black for you, Sam," said Tom. "Very black indeed."

Sam could not help but agree. Even if he could get back into the foundry, a life of drudgery lay before him. According to authority, there could be no escape. Everything was exactly as it had been explained to him at the National School. Then he thought of Victoria. Now she represented his true value. If only those shares had gone up instead of down, or if only he had bought some other shares. So much depends on luck, mused Sam. I just need a little luck. Perhaps I need not stay here after all. I was down on my luck before – next time everything will be different. Perhaps mother will not succeed in reinstating me into that place – then I shall be free to do as I wish. She will be looked after here – there are poor funds for deserving widows such as her. I do not believe that she needs me as much as she makes out. But I suppose I should not leave her alone all evening. I will just have another drink or two, then I shall go back home again. It was surely no more than four drinks later that Sam stepped out of The Red Lion again, much the better for them. As he ambled along, he saw approaching a young man of the cloth who could be none other than the Vicar of Bourton. It was no great coincidence, for the church at Bourton lay practically opposite. As the man came closer, he became uncannily familiar – until Sam fully realized that this was the vicar who had given such an inspiring sermon at Stoke Trister on the eve of his departure from home. The man seemed to know who he was, and stopped in front of him, viewing him with an alert expression.

"Would I be mistaken in thinking that you are Samuel Brazenall?"

"No, that is correct," said Sam.

"Your mother came and spoke to me this morning. She wished me to try to persuade William Maggs to reengage you. This I have already done. They are willing to take you on again, on apprentice wages."

"But I am fully qualified," said Sam.

"Nevertheless, you are back on trial. Should your work be satisfactory, your position will be reviewed."

"When do I start?" asked Sam, resignedly.

"I was intending to bring your mother the good news tomorrow," said the vicar. "But as you are here to hear it, I can save myself the journey. The sooner you start, the better. Tomorrow would be best."

"Tomorrow?"

"Yes, at 6 a.m."

"Right you are," said Sam.

"Perhaps I should introduce myself properly," said the man of the cloth. "I am the Reverend Clarendon, vicar of Bourton."

"How did you know who I was?" asked Sam.

"I never forget a face. A year or so ago, I had occasion to give a sermon at Stoke Trister, in place of their vicar, who was ill. You were sitting in the back pew with the rest of your family. And most attentive you were too, I am gratified to say."

"Normally I would sleep through a sermon," said Sam. "But I have to admit, you kept me awake. And it did not go on too long, either."

"Well, I am terrified of boring people," said the vicar. "So I keep my sermons as short and to the point as possible."

"Well, perhaps I shall come to hear you again," said

Sam. "But my family prefers the church at Stoke Trister. It is a mile closer, you see. And the walk to Bourton is uphill in places."

"Well, should they feel inclined to visit my church, they will be as welcome there as in Stoke Trister," said the vicar. "And if ever there is anything that you yourself wish to discuss with someone, I am always at your disposal."

"How did you become a vicar?" asked Sam, suddenly.

"I was appointed to the position by a relative," said the honoured man. Sam wondered what distant relatives he himself might have. Not that they would ever think of appointing him to anything.

"Well, thank you very much for what you have done for me," said Sam, finally. "I was a little worried that they might not take me back on again."

"Well, they may not the next time," said the Reverend. "This could be your last chance to make a living as a foundry worker."

"Yes," agreed Sam. It felt strange to think that tomorrow he would be back in the place that a year and a half ago he was so sure that he had left behind him. Strange and not entirely uplifting.

"Well, I am sure I will see you as I go around," said Sam. "Good evening. I will tell my mother the good news. I am sure she will be most relieved."

"Good night, Sam." The vicar went on past him. Sam hurried across the roadway and back to the inn. If he was going to work tomorrow, he would have to make the most of what remained of the evening.

*

The following morning, Sam rose at dawn. With little ceremony, he threw on his worn clothes and tramped into the kitchen. There he collected his eating bag and canister of coffee put out unfailingly by his mother. Then he hurried out into the road, walking towards the sun in a clear sky that depressed him. He walked quickly, now remembering everything as it used to be until he reached Bourton and the Factory Hill. There his footsteps became wearier; it was in disbelief that he finally entered the premises of Oliver Maggs, iron founder, and beheld the gloomy interior. He was met by his two overseers, in the form of Aaron and Mr Exon. Neither of them appeared to have aged a day. What am I doing back here, he asked himself. For a few moments, they did not speak but merely stared at him in a kind of morbid fascination. Everything was the same as he had left it; the sad, dirty men in work clothes, who hardly looked at him, the crane which served to lift the heaviest moulding boxes and the unfittingly elegant cupola at the back of the foundry.

"So you decided to come back to us," said Mr Exon, finally.

"I have no choice," said Sam. "My mother is widowed."

"Yes, well, I'm afraid we can't pay you a journeyman's wage," said Mr Exon. "You'll have to go back to apprentice wages for a while. That is, enough to cover your food and lodging."

"I'm very grateful," said Sam. They were being very reasonable.

"If, in time, you prove yourself worthy, well, then we will review your situation," went on Mr Exon. "But for now, Aaron is once again your overseer. You will be expected to regard him as such."

"Yes, of course."

"Well, that's it for now." Mr Exon walked out of the foundry.

For a few moments, Sam stared uncomprehendingly at Aaron. The man was not looking at him.

"You can start working over there," said Aaron, carelessly indicating a dark corner. "Start doing the moulds. That is if you still remember how to do them."

"Yes, I think I can just about remember," said Sam. It was all coming back to him too familiarly. He was now working on the parts for the range of 'handy motors' that the foundry was so proud of producing. He sifted a light covering of French chalk into the mould in front of him. I just don't believe that this is happening, he thought, as he picked up the shovel and began heaving in sand from the mass of it that lay beside him. At least I am still strong. Life on the road has not weakened me. And mother expects and desires that I should work. I have done the moulding process so many times that I can now do it in my sleep, with no concentration. I know where my next meal is coming from, and it won't be turnips or workhouse fodder. Surely this is an easier life? Yet a voice within told him that it was not. Even were you to find a wife, said the voice, she would not be like Victoria. Iron founders do not marry Victorias. What have you got yourself into?

Time seemed to have stopped. Aaron exchanged no unnecessary words with him. The air inside the foundry was as stuffy as ever before. I wonder if this air is at all good for my lungs, he considered, sensitively. Mr Exon certainly spends as little time in here as possible. He always seems to be in the machine shop. It is also uncommonly dark in here; one can hardly see what one is doing; he moved onto the second mould, then the third, then the fourth and fifth; after that, he stopped counting.

By mid-morning, they were ready for casting. As Sam walked across the foundry floor, carrying one end of the ladle containing the extremely bright molten iron, another thought struck him; was it really good for the eyes to look at such a blinding light? He had once been told by an old man never to look directly at the sun. Well, the liquid in the ladle seemed as bright as the sun. But he had to look at it when he and Aaron poured it carefully into each and every mould. And flashes appeared in front of him when he finally looked away. No, it could not possibly be advisable. Only a working-class man would be expected to do such a thing.

The sound of the dinner bell ringing out in the neighbouring flax mill did little to uplift him. Sitting by the factory pond in the pure air outside it was now clear that foundry life had not improved; the repetitive motions that before had been barely tolerable were now intolerable. Aaron was exactly the same as before. Yet the day had only just begun. Ten long hours stood between him and The Red Lion. He heard birds singing in the neighbouring trees, the wind rustling and the mill brook, and considered that there was nothing worse than being cooped up inside. His thoughts wandered to where he would rather be. Not in England, that was for sure. He had seen and done England; and there was the whole world remaining.

Paris! Now there was a city of dreams. Surely a romantic existence was promised if he could only get there. He turned out his pockets; the few remaining pence he found there would pay for a ship to the coast of France; from there he would walk on to the capital. This time everything would go right; he would make sure of that. No doubt there were beggars there too, but he would not be one of them. A more aggressive approach was in order. People went to Paris to paint, he had been told; well, he could not be an artist, but perhaps he could be a photographer; or maybe an artist's model. It was clear to him that Paris was not a place of work, but of artistry.

The factory bell was ringing out again. But Sam did not troop back inside. As soon as all the people had disappeared he trooped away back down factory hill, under the shade of the trees in the late April sunshine. He crossed the bridge over the mill stream and came back onto the highway. The sound of the mill machinery became gradually fainter. He was unsympathetic to the idea of returning home first and decided that he would leave Mr Exon to explain to his mother what had happened. Perhaps Mr Exon could even consider employing his mother in his place – if she was strong enough to carry water around in an iron pail, she was strong enough to shovel sand into a mould. Why should only men work outside the home? But such contemplation soon departed from his clearing head as he turned into the road that would eventually lead on to Southampton, whereupon the feeling of absolute and total freedom overcame him once more.